Infinity in the Palm of Her Hand

Also by Gioconda Belli

FICTION

The Scroll of Seduction
The Inhabited Woman

NONFICTION

The Country Under My Skin

POETRY

From Eve's Rib

INFINITY IN THE PALM OF HER HAND

A Novel of Adam and Eve

Gioconda Belli

Translated from the Spanish
by MARGARET SAYERS PEDEN

HARPER

An Imprint of HarperCollinsPublishers
www.harpercollins.com

INFINITY IN THE PALM OF HER HAND. Copyright © 2009 by
Gioconda Belli. Translation copyright © 2009 by Margaret Sayers
Peden. All rights reserved. Printed in the United States of America. No
part of this book may be used or reproduced in any manner whatso-
ever without written permission except in the case of brief quotations
embodied in critical articles and reviews. For information, address
HarperCollins Publishers, 10 East 53rd Street, New York, NY 10022.

HarperCollins books may be purchased for educational, business, or
sales promotional use. For information, please write: Special Markets
Department, HarperCollins Publishers, 10 East 53rd Street,
New York, NY 10022.

FIRST EDITION

Originally published in Spanish as *El infinito en la palma de la mano* by
Seix Barral, an imprint of Planeta Publishers in Spain.

Designed by Emily Cavett Taff

Library of Congress Cataloging-in-Publication Data is available upon
request.

ISBN: 978-0-06-167364-1

09 10 11 12 13 OV/RRD 10 9 8 7 6 5 4 3 2 1

This book is dedicated to the anonymous victims of the Iraq war.

Once upon a time, somewhere in the land between the Tigris and the Euphrates, there was a Paradise.

*And Babylon will become a heap of ruins, a haunt of jackals,
an object of horror and hissing, without inhabitants.*

—JEREMIAH 51:37

*And the end of all our exploring will be to arrive where we started
And know the place for the first time.*

—T. S. ELIOT

*To see a world in a grain of sand
And a heaven in a wild flower,
Hold infinity in the palm of your hand
And eternity in an hour.*

—WILLIAM BLAKE

AUTHOR'S NOTE

*W*HILE WAITING FOR my husband at the library in his father's house in Virginia, I came upon an old collection of books I had never noticed. I knew that my father-in-law had been unpacking boxes of books that had been stored in a warehouse for years, and I became curious. These books looked ancient. Dust had joined with their yellow leaves and hard brown covers; the spines were dry and brittle. Among them was a fourteen-volume work titled *Sacred Books and Literature of the East*. Some were dedicated to Babylon, to Egypt, and to China, but the title of the last volume caught my eye: *The Secret Books*.

Like many of you, raised in the Christian tradition, I was familiar with the story of Adam and Eve ever since I could remember. It never occurred to me, however, to wonder about what happened to them once they were expelled from Paradise. Yet inside *The Secret Books* I found *The Life of Adam and Eve*, a book that began exactly at that moment, and told the story of the trials and tribulations they faced once they were stripped of their privileges and left alone in a hostile and uncertain world.

What I read in that book fueled my imagination. I set off to find out more about the apocryphal versions of Genesis and the history of Creation. In my research I discovered that *The Life of Adam and Eve* dates as far back as the Bible we know today. Apocryphal books such as this were not included in the "official version" of the Book or the ecclesiastical canon. Centuries ago, the Church Fathers, for reasons unknown, decided to leave them out. The study of such writings has been left to academics or archaeologists who, through the ages, have discovered more of these ancient books, written in parchment and hidden inside jars in caves in the Middle East. Such is the case of the Dead Sea Scrolls, or the scrolls from Nag Hammadi.

Only the commentaries made to the Torah since antiquity by wise and learned rabbis, known as midrash, make use of this apocryphal approach to clarify or reflect upon the mysterious meanings and contradictions in Genesis and other biblical works.

To Adam and Eve, Genesis dedicates only forty verses. After reading the many apocryphal versions of their lives and the life of their descendants, including the surprising Luluwa and Aklia, Cain and Abel's twins, I decided to write this novel.

To imagine the first man and the first woman discovering themselves and discovering life around them, to wonder what they would feel, think, and experience—about their joys and sorrows—ended up as not only a poetic, literary exercise but also a deep exploration of my own humanity, of the myths that shape us and the way we cling to them, despite the truths science sets before us.

This novel is not Creationism, it's not Darwinism. It is fiction. Fiction based in the many fictions humankind has woven around this story since time immemorial. It is a close look at the difficult and dazzling beginning of our species. A recounting of the questions Adam and Eve might have asked themselves and that are paradoxically similar to those we continue to ask ourselves many eons later.

Part 1

MALE AND FEMALE
HE CREATED THEM

CHAPTER 1

*A*ND HE WAS.

Suddenly. From not being to being conscious that he was. He opened his eyes.

He touched himself and knew he was a man, without knowing how he knew. He saw the garden and he felt someone watching him. He looked in every direction hoping to see another like himself.

As he was looking, air spilled into his throat and its coolness stirred his senses. He could smell. He took a deep breath. In his head he felt the confused whirling of images seeking a name. Words, sounds, surged up inside him, clean and clear, and settled on everything around him. He named, and saw what he named recognize itself. The breeze moved the branches of the trees. A bird sang. Long leaves opened their finely drawn hands. Where was he? he asked. Why didn't the one who was watching allow himself to be seen? Who was this Other?

He walked, unhurried, until he had completed the circle

of the place where he had come to be. The greens, the forms and colors of the vegetation, filled the landscape and flowed into his gaze, and he felt a happiness in his chest. He named the stones, the streams, the rivers, the mountains, the cliffs, the caves, the volcanoes. He observed small things so as not to overlook them: the bee, moss, clover. At times, so much beauty left him dazed, unable to move: the butterfly, the lion, the giraffe. The steady beat of his heart accompanied him, independent of his wishing or knowing, a steady rhythm whose purpose was not his to divine. On his hands he experienced the warm breath of the horse, the coolness of water, the harshness of sand, the slippery scales of the fish, the soft fur of the cat. From time to time he looked up suddenly, hoping to surprise the Other, whose presence was softer than the wind though similar to it. The intensity of his gaze, however, was unequivocal. He sensed it on his skin, just as he perceived the unchanging, ever-present light that enveloped the Garden and illuminated the sky with its resplendent breath.

After he had done everything he thought he should do, the man sat on a stone to be happy and to contemplate it all. Two animals, a cat and a dog, came and lay at his feet. He tried to teach them to speak, but to no avail; they just looked longingly into his eyes.

Happiness seemed long-lasting and a bit monotonous to him. He could not touch it. He could not find a use for his hands. The birds flew past him swiftly, and very high. So did the clouds. All around him animals were grazing and drinking. He ate the white petals that fell from the sky. He needed nothing, and nothing seemed to need him. He was lonely.

He touched his nose to the ground and breathed in the

scent of grass. He closed his eyes and saw concentric circles of light beneath his eyelids. Lying on his side, he felt the moist earth inhale and exhale, imitating the sound of his respiration. A soft, silken drowsiness came over him. He surrendered to the sensation. Later he would remember his body opening, the split that divided his being to release the intimate creature that until then had dwelled within him. He could scarcely move. His body in its incarnation as chrysalis acted on its own; he could do nothing but wait in his state of semiconsciousness for whatever was to happen. If anything was clear, it was the extent of his ignorance; his mind filled with visions and voices for which he had no explanation. He stopped questioning himself and abandoned himself to the heavy sensation of his first sleep.

He awoke and remembered being unconscious. He found it entertaining to examine the faculties of memory, amusing himself by forgetting and remembering, until he saw the woman at his side. He lay very still, observing her bewilderment, the gradual effect of air in her lungs, of light in her eyes, the fluid way she moved to recognize herself. He imagined what she was going through, the slow awakening from nothingness to being.

He extended his hand and she held out hers, opened. Their palms touched. They measured their hands, arms, legs. They examined their similarities and their differences. He took her to walk through the Garden. He felt useful, responsible. He showed her the jaguar, the centipede, the raccoon, the turtle. They played; they watched the clouds roll by and change their shapes, they listened to the unvarying tune of the trees; they tried out words for describing what could not be named. He knew himself to be Adam, and he knew her as Eve. She wanted to know everything.

"What are we doing here?" she asked.

"I don't know."

"Who can explain to us where we came from?"

"The Other."

"Where is this Other?"

"I don't know where he is. I know only that he is all around."

She decided to look for him. She, too, had felt that she was being observed. They would have to climb to high places. She thought the look must come from there. Might it not be a bird? Perhaps, he said, admiring her astuteness. Walking among fragrant bushes and trees with generous foliage, without hurrying, they reached the highest volcano. They climbed it and from the top saw the green circle of the Garden, surrounded on all sides by thick whitish fog.

"What is that farther up?" she asked.

"Clouds," he answered.

"And behind the clouds?"

"I don't know."

"Maybe that's where the one who's observing us lives. Have you tried to go outside the Garden?"

"No. I know we are not supposed to go any farther than where it's green."

"How do you know that?"

"I just know."

"The way you knew the names?"

"Yes."

It did not take long for Eve to reach the conclusion that

the gaze of whatever was watching them did not belong to a bird. The enormous phoenix, with its red and blue feathers, had whirled above them, but like the rest of the creatures, had merely glanced toward them.

"Maybe it's that tree," she ventured, pointing toward the center of the Garden. "Look, Adam, look at it. Its canopy brushes the clouds as if it were playing with them. Maybe the one that sees us lives beneath its shade, or maybe what we feel is the gaze of the trees. There are so many, and they are everywhere. It may be that they are like us, except that they don't talk or move."

"The one observing us moves," said Adam. "I have heard his footsteps in the foliage."

They made their way down the volcano, wondering what to do to find the Other.

Eve began to call him. Adam was astounded that such a deep moan could issue from her, a lament of the air in her unwinged body. She had gone to stand at the bank of the river, with her arms opened wide. Her dark hair fell down her back. Her distant and perfect profile, her face with the closed eyes and open mouth from which that invocation issued, moved Adam. He asked himself whether they were wasting their time imagining an Other like them hidden deep in the luxuriant vegetation, where it was impossible to distinguish one tree from another. But both Adam and the woman had sensed not only his gaze but also his voice, whispering to them in the language that, more and more fluently, they used to communicate. And they even thought they had seen his watching shadow reflected in the eyes of the dog and the cat. Adam wondered if maybe they would see him when their eyes were more mature, less new. They still had difficulty distinguishing what existed only in their minds from what they observed around them. Eve especially was prone to confusing the one with the other. She claimed she had seen more than one animal with a human head and chest, lizards that flew, women of water.

From beyond the confines of the Garden they often heard the sound of cataclysms. They saw distant darkness and intermittent eruptions, streams of comets blazing across the firmament. Yet above them the sky remained unchanged, glowing with a golden clarity whose tones increased or diminished in no predictable order. When the earth quivered beneath their feet, Eve would tiptoe toward Adam, playing at not losing her balance. He would watch her, entranced, the toes of her feet stretching and contracting, reminding him of fishes.

Adam did not remember the tree in the center of the Garden. He thought it was strange that he hadn't noted it before, since he believed he had explored the place from end to end.

"The one watching us does not want to be seen. He is protecting himself, but we must find him, Adam. We must know why he is observing us, what it is he expects us to do."

Adam decided they would follow the course of one of the rivers. They walked into the humid jungle. Their nostrils were filled with the heavy, penetrating odors of the fertile soil where all sorts of ferns and mushrooms and orchids grew. The graceful, complex nests of golden orioles swung from the high branches from which lichens and mosses spilled like lace above their heads. They saw sleeping sloths hanging by their tails. Groups of raucous monkeys peered at them as they pirouetted through the treetops. Tapirs, wild pigs, and rabbits crossed their path, brushing against their legs in a friendly manner. Though the warm heart of encompassing green welcomed them, throbbing with life, they walked in silence, soaking up the atmosphere filled with the sounds and aromas of the hidden heart of their Paradise.

The jungle was so dense that they walked in circles and lost their way again and again, but they persisted. At last they came out in the center of the Garden. They discovered that this was the origin of all the paths that radiated from here and later forked, and of the two rivers that flowed to the east and the west. They found an enormous tree; beneath its trunk earth and water were joined together. As it stretched upward, its branches disappeared into the clouds, and they extended farther to all sides than their eyes could see. Adam felt an impulse to bow before its magnificence. Eve went straight to the tree. Instinctively Adam tried to stop her, but she turned and looked at him with an air of pity.

"It can't move," she told him. "It doesn't speak."

"It hasn't moved. It hasn't spoken," he said. "But we don't know what it's capable of doing."

"It's a tree."

"Not just any tree. It is the Tree of Life."

"How do you know?"

"The moment I saw it, I knew."

"It is very beautiful."

"Imposing. And I would say that you should not get so close."

Although the tree seemed to paralyze him, she could barely contain her desire to touch its broad and robust, its soft and gleaming, trunk. Beauty flooded her eyes everywhere, and the man had proudly showed her a myriad of colors and birds and majestic beasts, but to her nothing seemed more beautiful than the tree. Its leaves filled her imagination. They were lustrous, their backs painted a luminous green that contrasted with the underside, which was purple with thick, bright, salient veins. Arrayed on the many branches, extending in every direction, the leaves swallowed the light and then exhaled it, distributing radiance all about them. The skin of the round, white fruit shone, caught in the scintillating phosphorescence that radiated from the tree toward every part of the Garden. As Eve approached, the fruit-scented breath of the great tree tingled like unfamiliar excitement in her mouth, a current of life that was transmitted throughout the surroundings. Like Adam, she was overcome with reverence, and she had second thoughts about her initial impulse to touch the bark and eat the fruit. She was very close, and the crinkled skin was within reach of her hand, when her eyes lighted on a twin image. It was as if she were seeing a reflection in a pond: another, identical, tree rising before her, strange and complicit. Everything that was light about the first tree was crepuscular in the second: purple on the back of the leaves, green on the reverse, the fig fruit dark. It was wrapped in dense air and a dull, opaque light.

Adam, who had kept hidden, observing her, moved closer when she circled the great round trunk and disappeared behind it.

Even when he heard her, he still could not see her. He wondered whom she could be talking with. Until then, they had not come across any other creature that could put into words the sensations of the body. The cat, the dog, and the rest of the animals communicated in elementary melodies. If hearing her intrigued him, seeing the tree reproduced in an identical image with inverted colors left him stunned. Carefully, not making a sound, he followed the murmur of her words. He saw her seated on an enormous root that sank into the earth as if it were one of the extremities of what he imagined might be the reflection of how the Tree of Life thought of itself. Perhaps instead of talking, he told himself, the tree sees what it imagines. He was about to step out into the open, around the broad trunk, when he heard a voice. He thought that the Other had finally allowed himself to be seen; but then he was assailed by doubt. This voice did not sound like the disembodied one whose murmurs he knew, the one that light as the air had the quality of resonating inside his chest. This was like liquid slipping along the earth and dragging stones as it went. He heard its laughter. It laughed like the woman. It said:

"So! You noticed that we were observing you. How perceptive of you! And you have devoted yourselves to looking for us? Excellent! I suspected that would happen, but I am happy to know it was so. We could not resist the desire to watch you. It has been very entertaining."

"You are not alone, then? Do you have a companion too?"

"Companion? Me? Mmmm I never thought of it in that way."

"But there is someone else, besides you?"

"Elokim. He is the one who created you."

"The man says I came out of him."

"You were hidden inside him. Elokim placed you on one of his ribs. Not inside his head, so that you would not know pride, and not in his heart, so that you would never feel the desire to possess."

Those were its words. Adam kept listening.

"What is there beyond this Garden; why are we here?"

"Why do you want to know? You have everything you need."

"Why would I *not* want to know? What does it matter if I know?"

"Only Elokim knows the reason for everything that exists. If you should eat of the fruit of this tree, then you would know as well. You would be like him. You would understand the reason for all things. That is why I am here, at the foot of the Tree of Knowledge of Good and Evil, to warn you not to partake of these fruits, because if you do you will loose your innocence and die." The creature smiled maliciously.

Eve wondered what this creature was made of. Her skin was different from theirs, iridescent and flexible, composed of small scales, like the scales of fish. She was tall, and her body, curving and graceful, flowed into long, flexible arms and legs. Two golden, sparkling, almond-shaped eyes protruded from her smooth, almost flat face, and the straight slit of her mouth was fixed in an expression of ironic complacency and composure. Instead of hair, her head was covered with white feathers.

"Elokim prefers that you remain tranquil and passive, like the cat and the dog. Knowledge causes disquiet, nonconformity. One ceases to be capable of accepting things as they are and tries to change them. Look what he did himself. In seven days he drew from Chaos all that you see here. He conceived the Earth, and created it: the skies, water, plants, animals. And last, he made the two of you: a man and a woman. Today he is resting. Eventually he will be bored. He will not know what to do, and again I will be the one who has to soothe him. That is how it has been through Eternity. Constellation after constellation. He conceives and then forgets his creations."

Hidden behind the tree, Adam followed the dialogue between Eve and the creature, filled with curiosity. His chest felt tight and his breathing was rapid. He remembered murmurs from the Other warning him of something about a tree. Do not go near it. Do not touch it. No clear explanation of why he did not want them to do that. Until now the only obligation that made sense to Adam was that he was to accompany the woman, though she could easily care for herself. The same was true of the Garden. The plants grew and adapted in their own way without his intervention. The tone of the creature that was talking with Eve sounded vaguely familiar. It was the tone he had used to question himself about the designs of the Other. It was similar to the sound of his impatience when he tried to understand the reason for being.

"So you think that it's that simple," Eve was saying. "I bite into the fruit from this tree and I will know everything I want to know."

"And you will die."

"I don't know what that is. It doesn't worry me."

"You are very young for it to worry you."

"And you, why is it that you know all this?"

"I have existed much longer than you. I told you, I have seen all this created. And not even I know what its meaning is. Elokim creates infinite permutations from nothingness. He gives them great importance."

"But not you?"

"I find it a futile exercise not entirely devoid of arrogance."

"Do you think we are a caprice of the one you call Elokim?"

"In truth, I do not know. Sometimes it seems to me that it is. What meaning does your existence have? Why did he create you? You will eventually be bored in this Garden."

"Adam believes that we will work the land, and that we will care for the plants and the animals."

"What is there to care for? What labor is there to be done? Everything is done. Everything functions perfectly." The creature suppressed a yawn. "Adam and you, however, unlike all the other creatures of the universe, have the freedom to choose what you want. You are free to eat or not to eat of the fruit of this tree. Elokim knows that History will begin only when you use your freedom, but you know already that he is afraid you will use it; he fears that his creations might end up being too much like Him. He would rather contemplate the eternal reflection of his innocence. That is why he has forbidden you both to decide to be free and eat from the Tree. It may be that freedom is not what either of you would choose. You see, the very idea paralyzes you."

"It seems that you want me to eat this fruit."

"No. I merely envy the fact that you have the option of choosing. If you eat of the fruit, you and Adam will be free like Elokim."

"Which would you choose? Knowledge or eternity?"

"I am a serpent. The Serpent. I told you that I do not have the option to choose."

Eve looked at the tree. What would change if she bit into one of those fruits? Why believe what the Serpent told her? And yet, she did not dare take the step to test it. She looked at her hands, moved her long fingers one by one.

"I will be back," she said.

CHAPTER 2

*L*YING IN THE SUN AFTER A SWIM, THE MAN AND THE woman both withdrew into themselves. What can Adam be thinking? Eve asked herself. What can Eve be thinking? Adam wondered.

But neither of them was able to penetrate the thoughts of the other. Resting on the grass, they watched ants constructing an underground nest, carrying small leaves on their backs and marching in an orderly file toward the hole in the ground that would be their refuge. All around them the greenery was dazzling, interrupted here and there by bursts of color from flower-laden branches and bushes. The two rivers that cut across the Garden divided into four tributaries. They were lying on the bank of the quietest of these, one that flowed from a higher elevation. The slopes along its course were studded with enormous, polished, gray-green boulders that forced the current to slow, grow calm, and sing as it ran among verdant conifers and a blanket of ferns with large toothed leaves. Eve breathed in the scent of growing things and felt the warm breeze blow over her delicately and pleasurably, drying her body. Adam, too, had abandoned himself to the sensation of the wind, the Garden's smell of vegetation, the sounds from the huge black bear playing on the opposite shore. Overhead, the trees were murmuring in their leafy tongue. On one low branch, a canary was cleaning its feathers with its beak. From time to time there burst from its throat a high, brilliant melody that seemed to contain the essence of every living sound.

What had the Serpent meant when she stated that history would begin only when they used their freedom? Why did she say that she was envious that they could choose? Why would she say they should not eat from the Tree of Knowledge if at the same time she was urging them to do it? What was her connection with the Other? What was the Other afraid for them to know? Eve could not answer that riddle. Above all else, she did not understand why this Elokim had decided to entice her as he had. Why lead her to the tree, imprint in her bones the way to find it, reveal its presence in the center of the Garden? If it had not been for her, Adam would never have gone there. He would never have seen those trees. He himself had told her so when he admired her curiosity and the intuition that had guided her to them.

She looked at Adam, stretched out on the grass with his arm folded over his eyes, his chest rhythmically rising and falling. He was a large man, tall, and the lines of his body were simple, straight, devoid of curvature; only the swell of his muscles had any resemblance to the roundness that predominated in hers. She wondered whether Elokim had carved him from some slab taken from the mountain, and whether he had made her smaller and softer in order not to cause the man pain when he took her out of him. Had he modeled her thinking of the shape of a fruit? A hill? She would have liked to know.

Adam thought it was almost possible for him to hear what she was mulling over. What could he do to keep her away from the Tree? Docility was not in her nature. The best thing about her was her inability to stay still, the vivacity with which she examined and questioned everything from the start.

It rained. Along with the rain came the white petals that fell from the sky to nourish them. He taught her how to pull a leaf from the banana tree and hold it open until it was spilling over with petals. After the shower a rainbow appeared. It looked like a bridge between heaven and Earth, he said, though he had never seen anyone cross it.

"Why is it that the creature at the tree, the one called Serpent, has seen Elokim and we haven't?" Eve wanted to know.

"Strange that she named herself," Adam said thoughtfully

"You don't think that she is Elokim?"

Adam looked at her, astonished that she could think such a thing.

"But why couldn't she be? She seems to know everything the Other thinks," Eve insisted.

"Maybe she is his reflection."

"You said that we are his reflection."

"You mean, the way that the Tree of Knowledge is the reflection of the Tree of Life?"

"I suppose so."

"But if we are his reflection then the Serpent can't be. She doesn't look like us."

"So we will have our very own reflection?"

"I don't know, Eve. You ask a lot of questions I cannot

answer. I will continue to look for the Other. You stay here. Do not talk with the Serpent anymore. Try to calm down. You seem agitated."

Eve went to the edge of the water. Her feet led her downstream. The water in the river was clear and among the rocks glittered the scales of multicolored fish. One large red fish with black and white spots around its mouth was swimming with determination toward a bend in the river where the water looked very quiet. Eve followed it. She climbed up on a black stone that jutted above the pool and sat there to watch the fish as it moved swiftly in the depths of the river without disturbing its calm. A bubble rose from the bottom of the pool, and from out of nowhere came an enormous eye that opened its eyelashes and looked at her, and as it did allowed her to see through its crystalline iris a succession of dizzying and fascinating images. She watched herself biting into the fig, and then, evolving from that seemingly irrelevant incident, came a gigantic spiral of ephemeral and transparent men and women who multiplied and spread across magnificent landscapes, their faces alight with a myriad of expressions, their skins reflecting shades from the gleam of wet tree trunks to the pale petals of the rhododendron. Around them swirled shapes and forms, unnamed objects among which they moved with aplomb and without haste, inquisitive and curious, as they unveiled a multiplicity of visions that in turn split into bottomless depths, strata of incomprehensible symbols whose meaning they debated in an onslaught of confused sounds and harmonies whose echoes nevertheless resonated inside Eve, as if by not knowing them she knew them. In the accelerating spin of these succeeding cycles, she saw them, hidden and confused, burn and twist, light and extinguish terrible conflagrations from which they emerged again and again. Their faces were tirelessly renewed, repeated in the incessant motion of that animated and cacophonous multitude spilling across never-seen lands, unknown places, gesticulating, displaying emotions that rippled or floated on the water that reflected them, emotions in which she perceived the same thirst for knowledge that consumed her, as well as profound currents and perplexities she would have liked to be able to name. To peer into that energetic and unrelenting tumult, to glimpse the unknown spaces, to hear the murmur of her blood respond to a vulnerable and shared destiny, inspired in her a tenderness and a desire deeper than anything she had known until then. Curiously, the last image that emerged before the water stilled was so placid and clear that she wondered whether it was she herself realizing she was still in the Garden, or whether the mystery at the end of it all was the possibility of going back to the beginning.

History, Eve said to herself. She had seen it. That was what would begin if she ate of the fruit. Elokim wanted her to decide whether or not it existed. He did not want to be responsible for it. He wanted her to be the one to bear that onus.

CHAPTER 3

*E*VE RAN TO LOOK FOR ADAM. SHE DID NOT FIND him in the meadow, where he liked to teach the dog to obey and to intuit his thoughts. She did not find him in the lush jungle, or back on the bank of the river. Weary, she stopped and sat down on the grass. She looked around with nostalgia, as if she were seeing a memory. She saw greenness, water, and blue mountains.

What was the difference between the images she had seen in the water and others that often were revealed to her as she strolled through isolated areas of the Garden, alone, without Adam's presence at her side to stand between her and her imagination? Adam said that the fabulous creatures that appeared to her where the golden light barely filtered through the dense vegetation were visions: women of water playing with butterflies with tiny human faces and long manes, birds discussing the world with animals that had human torsos, enormous leaves on which hieroglyphics appeared and disappeared, gigantic creatures that fed on the dense clouds they tore from the sky, the lizard that spat fire as it followed a body so long that, even though its own, it attacked as if it belonged to another.

Unlike those iridescent, evanescent visions, the ones she saw in the river were strong, clear, their reality more forceful than that of the Garden itself. She had been allowed to see them, she thought, not merely to share in the all-enveloping gaze that came from within Elokim, but to experience the abundance of life that filled him in such profusion that it overflowed and was transformed, perhaps mocking his will, into creation bursting from a wish before he had time to repent. However much this life might defy him, he must be fascinated to witness the destiny of beings that, perhaps moved by what the Serpent called freedom, contrived to go against and live outside his creative will. This could be the reason why he was inciting her to bring that other world into existence. His curiosity to see those beings creating and destroying themselves and each other might be as irresistible to him as it was to her.

The man would think that she had seen visions induced by the Serpent to motivate her to disobey the command not to eat of the Tree of Knowledge of Good and Evil. He would not believe her when she told him that unless she dared disturb the tranquillity of the Garden, uncounted creatures would not otherwise exist. They themselves would end up simply as the dream of an ingenious dreamer who imagined free creatures and then confined them to live as flowers or birds.

Her nature refused to accept that the only purpose for Adam's and her existence was to be lulled in the contemplation of that eternity in which tranquillity had of late been changed into tense expectation, with the alert gaze of the Other constantly on her. The Serpent was mistaken in believing that when they bit into the fruit of the Tree they would be like Elokim. Just the opposite. They would cease to be like him. They would separate themselves from him. They would initiate history, do what they had been created to do: they would found a species, they would people a planet, they would explore the limits of consciousness and reason. Only she, using that freedom, could provide Elokim with the experience of Good and Evil he so desired. It was so they would take creation in their own hands that he had made Adam and her in his image and likeness.

But since Adam had not seen what she had been allowed to observe, he would not understand either the Other's games or her determination. Asked to choose, perhaps he would opt for the immutable eternity of the Garden. She would have to do it alone, she told herself. She sat in a quiet place beside the pool to listen to the bubbling of her ideas. Doubt and determination were opposing currents rising and falling in her body. When she closed her eyes she could see the river's images. Why should she be the one to discover what was hidden behind the Other's prohibition? Why was she the one chosen to shatter the mirage of the Garden? Who are you, Elokim? Where are you? When will you show us your face?

She got up and started back toward the center of the Garden, toward the Tree of Knowledge of Good and Evil, where the Serpent would be waiting.

CHAPTER 4

*T*HE SERPENT'S SMILE WAS SWEET AND IRONIC WHEN she saw Eve emerge from the dense vegetation.

"You're back very soon," she said.

"Are there other gardens or is this the only one?"

The Serpent smiled. "May I ask to what a question like that is owed?"

"In the depths of the river I saw strange images that seemed more real than you or I or all this. I felt that it was my responsibility to make them exist."

"And what do you think you must do to make that happen?"

"I must use my freedom. Eat of the fruit."

"You're not afraid?"

"Elokim wants me to do it."

"That isn't what he told me."

"I know that, and I don't understand it."

"Perhaps he fears your freedom. The culmination of the

creator is to create his own challenge, but one never knows what Elokim intends. You can't say I didn't warn you. You could die—although I admit that it would be absurd for Elokim to destroy you so soon."

"I will not die. I know. He wants me to do it. That is why he made me free."

"You can decide not to do it."

"No. That would be too easy. That is no longer possible. I must have knowledge."

"You have to know." The Serpent laughed. "He truly did make you in his image and likeness. He is the one who knows everything."

"And the one who is afraid of knowing. But I am not afraid. I have seen too many things. Why would he have me see them if not to understand them and dare them to exist?"

"Maybe so you would accept that it isn't possible for you to understand everything."

Eve pondered that. She had crossed the meadow under the attentive gaze of the buffalo and the elephant that had begun to follow her. When she reached the center of the Garden and stood at the foot of the Tree, she saw that many animals had followed her, at once alarmed and fascinated. She looked all around. She wasn't even sure that she would have the courage to do what her conscience dictated, but she had no alternative. The entire Garden was waiting.

"First I will touch the tree. We will see if it's true that it will cause my death."

"Look at me. I am leaning against it, and nothing has happened to me. It is not so easy to die."

"I saw death and I did not like it. What will I feel if I die?"

"You will feel nothing. That is precisely the problem. You will never feel anything again. Death has a terrible simplicity." The Serpent smiled.

Eve hurried. Her hands were sweating. It seemed that the air had stopped moving. There was barely enough to fill her chest. She held out her right hand. She felt the vegetal skin of the Tree against her right palm. She wiggled her fingers. She heard the throbbing of her body, ready to burst. She closed her eyes. She opened them. She was still standing in the same place. She was alive. Nothing had changed. She was not going to die, she thought. She would eat and she would not die. Emboldened, she walked to a low branch and took one of the dark fruits in her hand. It was soft to the touch. She put it to her lips. She felt the sweetness of the fig along the length of her tongue; the smooth flesh spilled honey among her teeth. The ephemeral white petals that fell, light as foam, from the sky seemed no more than insubstantial matter compared with the penetrating juice and aroma of the forbidden fruit. She bit down. She felt the fragrance spread inside her. Pleasure from her taste buds reverberated through her body like an echo. She opened her eyes and saw the Serpent, still in the same position. The animals. Everything just the same. Greedy for more, she took another fruit. The nectar dribbled down her chin. She yielded to euphoria. She threw one fruit, then another and another, to the animals, defiant and content. The animals merged together. One by one they came toward her and drank the figs' juice from her hand. She wanted them all to eat; she wanted to share the new flavor, the sensation of for the first time doing what her body asked her to do. Not only had she not died; she felt more alive than ever. She heard the Phoenix swooping above her head. She called to it. She held out a fig. The bird did not descend. It flew away. In the distance she heard its sorrowful call.

Leaning against the trunk of the Tree, the Serpent stared at her without altering her usual ironic, composed expression, keeping her distance from the frenzy that had seized Eve and the animals.

Adam knew what it was the moment he heard the sound of revelry in the distance. His body stiffened. He walked faster. He feared he would find himself alone again, without a companion. He feared he would get there and find Eve struck down by Elokim's fury. He began to run. As he ran, a cold emptiness bored into his side. Without the woman, he would not be the same, he thought. If she, who was bone of his bones, flesh of his flesh, disappeared, he would wander incomplete and desolate. He had almost no past, and what he did have was filled with her.

Eve saw him coming. She trembled when she saw he was running toward her. His skin was covered with gleaming sweat. She noticed his strong legs, the thrust of his feet, his look of alarm. She crossed her hands over her breast. She faced him.

"I did it," she said. "I did it and I did not die. I gave the fruit to the animals and they did not die. Now, you must eat."

She held out a ripe fig. The man thought that she had never before looked at him like that. She implored him to eat it. He did not want to think. She was his flesh and his bones. It was not in him to leave her alone. He did not want to be left alone.

He bit into the fruit. He felt the sweet juice moisten his tongue, the soft flesh catch in his teeth. He closed his eyes and was struck dumb by the pleasure of the sensation.

He turned to look at her. Her back was to him. The arching curve of her waist lifted her handsomely round buttocks. He wondered whether if he bit them, they would taste as sweet as the fig. He reached out to feel that perfect roundness, amazed that he had never before noticed the exquisite softness of her skin. He pulled his hand back but the sensation lingered on his fingers, so strong and clear that it made him shiver. Eve turned, and he reached out again and touched the curve of her breast. The woman stared at him, long and hard. Her eyes were opened wide.

They heard the thudding hooves of the animals. They saw the herd of elephants milling about, the buffalo, the tigers, the lions. The air was filled with endless guttural sounds, howls, incomprehensible laments.

Adam looked at Eve. He experienced his first confusion.

Eve was staring at him. She wanted him to stop looking at her as if now that he had bitten the fruit he was thinking of biting her, eating her. She put her hands over her breasts.

"Stop looking at me," she said. "Don't look at me like that."

"I can't help it," he said. "My eyes do not obey my will."

"I will cover myself," she said, tearing leaves from the fig tree.

"I as well," he said, aware that, like him, she was not able to take her eyes from his legs, his hands, as if they were new to her.

Eve looked for the creature of the Tree of Knowledge. She

did not see her anywhere. She began to call her, until she saw her overhead, near the top of the tree.

"What are you doing there?"

"I'm hiding."

"Why?"

"Soon you will know. Soon you will know everything you have wanted to know."

CHAPTER 5

THE MAN WAS WALKING WITH LONG STRIDES. EVE hurried along behind him. He said that they should hide and wait for whatever was going to happen. He was frightened. She, on the other hand, was waiting for knowledge to be manifest. She tried to convince him that they should go look instead for the Other and tell him what they had done, ask him to tell them what more they had to do. How would they know Good and Evil? Was merely having eaten the fruit enough for them to tell one from the other? And if they did not recognize them? Look, I have only done my part, she argued. Now Elokim will have to do his, teach them all that they could be. But Adam did not want to listen to her. He had followed her to eat the fruit, he told her. Now she had to follow him. As they walked on, branches snapped and birds flew up from the trees. The earth smelled like rain. The Garden was still vibrant and unharmed. Light from the trees shed gold among the vines and trunks and foliage. No sound came from the animals. The man was barely speaking. Eve looked at his back. From his waist hung the fig leaves he had tied together with a vine. Eating the fruit had awakened a strange hunger in her. Hunger for sweet juices, for running her lips over Adam's skin. Her senses were keenly aware of the air, the leaves, and she wanted to touch everything with her hands. Adam said nothing, but she watched how he was examining the details of the path and stopping to sniff the air. He had looked at her as if he needed to brush against her, know her with the awareness of a newly discovered body.

Adam did not want to tell the woman what he was feeling. He hadn't as yet found a way to explain it to himself. Ever since he'd bitten into the fruit, nothing he did had coherence. His bizarre vitality was a wall between him and tranquillity. He was conscious of the weight of his bones, the flexibility of his muscles, the revealed design of his movements; he perceived the earth, the dust, the moisture on the soles of his feet. He could not decide whether he preferred this new sentience over his habitual serenity, whether he preferred the slow pace of his existence over the determination and clarity of purpose that now were leading him to the slit in the rock he had discovered during one of his explorations. As never before, he knew what he wanted, but fear restrained his exuberance. He was sure of one thing. He and Eve had not died. Could it be true what Eve thought? Could Elokim be relieved?

He guided Eve through the purple passion flowers that fell in clusters over the partially hidden entrance. She slipped nimbly through and emitted an admiring exclamation when she stepped inside the cave and saw its walls of quartz. The rose and crystal of the minerals glowed, lit by the sun filtering through an opening high in the wall of rock. From the depths of the cave came the sound of running water. It was a beautiful place, she said, walking toward the back as far as the limits of the light. It would be more difficult for the Other to find them there, he said. If he knows everything he will find us, she said. At least we are at some distance from the Trees and the Serpent. But I can assure you that he will not kill us. Since he put us here, he has to have known what would happen. If the consequences were irreversible, he would not have created us. How could she be so sure, he asked, that the Other would not return them to nothingness once he realized they had acted against his wishes? The only thing Eve was sure of was that the Other was not that simple. It was enough to see his work. Everything that surrounded them was continually changing. The plants, the animals. As if each creature were but the beginning of other, different, more complex ones. I asked you, Adam, if we would have a reflection. And I saw it. In the river. Many like us will people the Earth, love, produce their own creations; they will be complicated and handsome. Adam smiled faintly. I hope so, he said. He dropped down on the fine gray sand of the cave floor and held out his hand to take hers and help her sit beside him. He put his arm around her shoulders. Eve snuggled close to his chest. They had sat that way many times, gazing at the river, the meadow, the rain in the lush jungle, but this time the need to be together, to have their skin touching, had a peculiar intensity. Eve buried her nose in his chest. She breathed in his scent. He put his hands in her hair and sniffed her in turn.

"It's strange," she said. "I am wishing I could get back inside your body, go back to the rib you say I came from. I am wishing for the skin that separates us to disappear." He smiled and pressed her closer to him. He wanted that, too, he said, touching his lips to her shoulder. He would like to eat her the way he had eaten the forbidden fruit. Eve smiled. She took Adam's hand and one by one guided his fingers to her mouth, pushing them inside, sucking them. His salty skin still held the flavor of the forbidden fig. He watched what she was doing with fascination, registering on his fingers the warm, juicy heat of her mouth, like an ocean mollusk. Could Eve have the ocean inside her? And did he as well? If not, what was that tide he felt suddenly rising in his groin, that spread from his legs and burst in his chest, making him moan? He withdrew his hand from that unbearable sensation and laid his head in the curve of Eve's neck. She lifted her head and sighed, and as she did her neck arched. He saw her closed eyes, and gently ran his hands over her breasts, awed by the smoothness, the color, the feel of the small rosy aureoles that abruptly grew hard beneath his fingertips, just like the taut skin of his penis that suddenly, as if moved by a will of its own, had lost it habitual lassitude to rise up like a disproportionate finger and unequivocally point to Eve's belly. She, her body tense, gave in to her desire to lick Adam all over. Soon, on the floor of the grotto, they were a sphere of legs and arms and hands and mouths among moans and muffled laugher, pursuing, stroking, exploring each other, slowly, marveling at what their bodies suddenly unfolded, the hidden moistness and unexpected erections, the magnetic effect of their mouths, lips, and tongues joining together like secret passages through which the sea of one exploded on the shore of the other. However much they touched, they could not sate their desire for more. They were sweating profusely, burning in their ardor, when Adam was struck by an uncontainable impulse to release the torrent rising from his center into Eve's body, and she, at last gifted with knowledge, knew that she must open an inner path for him, that it was toward there the surprising extremity that had suddenly appeared between Adam's legs was pointing. Finally, one inside the other, they experienced the rapture of once again being a single body. They knew that as long as they stayed that way, they would never again know loneliness. Even if words were to desert them and silence fill their minds, they would be able to lie together and say things to each other without speaking. They thought that this was undoubtedly the knowledge the Serpent had told them they would possess when they ate of the fruit of the Tree. Rocking together, arms around each other, they returned to nothingness, and their bodies, unbounded, were created anew to mark the beginning of the world and of History.

CHAPTER 6

$\mathcal{F}$OR THE SECOND TIME IN HIS LIFE, ADAM SLEPT. IN his sleep he saw an immense sphere bristling with spikes. The spikes were straight, upright trees. From each tree emerged the waist, torso, and head of a half-formed man or a half-formed woman. Each of these half-tree, half-human beings had clinging to its outstretched arms other men and other women, who formed the tops of that vast humanoid forest. One by one they were breaking off. They cracked and split and fell to the ground, expelling long laments. Adam flew above the throng of staring faces impotently contemplating him; their voices rang out in his heart, disconcerted by the terror of an end they could not comprehend. Adam flew on. He could not stop that circling flight; he could not stop the crashing of the dying trees.

He awoke trembling. He sat up beside Eve. He woke her. Outside he heard the vengeful, antagonistic roar of the wind. The Earth was convulsing. He thought that it must be the faint throbbing with which it sometimes declared itself alive, but he was troubled by the hostile energy with which they were being shaken; it was as if the Earth were attempting to rid itself of them. Eve looked at him with alarm. The cave where only recently they had lain in such happy reveling was being pummeled by a gigantic fist. Pieces of crystals and rosy quartz were breaking loose, shattering into bits when they fell. They were assaulted by hostile rocks and dust. The world of cataclysms and strayed comets whose noise had from time to time filtered into their evenings suddenly erupted beneath their feet. Adam, Adam! Could it be because we ate the fruit? I too saw our descendants, he yelled; they will live but because of our guilt they will die. One by one they will be broken off and they will fall, he moaned. He tried to get to his feet, to walk, but he was unable to find his balance. He fell again and again. Pieces of rocks kept raining down; the walls of the cave were bursting open. A dark cloud of dust enveloped them, forcing them to close their eyes. Eve buried her head in her arms. Like Adam, she tried to walk, and also like him, she fell with each attempt. Now they would die, she thought. Everything the Serpent had foretold would come to pass. Crawling, Adam succeeded in moving forward a short distance. He told her to do the same and follow him. Like an animal, she thought. On all fours like an animal, she followed. The Earth did not stop roaring, stop rocking and swaying. A large rock fell on Adam's leg. He yelled with pain, and she went to him and was able to free him from it. His leg was bleeding. They had never seen blood. They examined the wound. Fiery red was running in a small stream across his skin. We must get out of here, said Adam. They had to get out before the walls of the cave collapsed. My eyes, thought Eve, are so wide open they're burning. I'm afraid. Crawling, dragging themselves, they left the cave. Outside, the sky was dark; gray dust fell over the Earth, a solid rain that hurt the skin. They could barely see the chaos, the disorder in the Garden, the animals racing about, bawling and bleating. They heard the crash of uprooted trees, the terrible din of disaster that suddenly transformed them into small, vulnerable creatures, fragile and terrorized. A few meters away the earth opened along an invisible crack. Eve closed her eyes and yelled as loud as she could, thinking that the sound of her voice might calm the furor of the irate spirit intent on destroying everything. Adam squeezed his fists and told her to be quiet. It was Eve, he thought. Eve and her curiosity. He dragged her along the ground, as far as possible from the precipice that, with a deafening roar, was forming along the fissure. Pushing and crashing, the ground tore apart, split as if an invisible, all-powerful ray had cut through it, carving out a wide chasm. Eve did not want to see what she was seeing: the Garden moving off beyond their reach, rejecting them. When the ground stopped shaking, she saw the Garden of Eden recompose itself on the other side of the broad, deep abyss. She saw it return to its placidity and its golden light, like a strange island in the Earth. The Garden, she exclaimed to herself; she had never thought they would lose it, never thought that they would be left outside, separated, excluded.

Suddenly they felt a watery oscillation beneath their feet, as if below the surface of the earth a tide were moving the rocks, everything that only recently had been solid and rigid. Beside them abruptly appeared a strange, long creature with a round body and scaly skin, slithering along the ground. Eve recognized the face, the eyes.

"Is it you?"

"He has turned me into this. His mood will change. When he gets angry he does things he later forgets. Fortunately, when he remembers, he regrets what he's done and makes amends. What he's done to me won't last long, but in your case it will take much longer. You will never be able to return to the Garden."

"It's your fault," said Adam, recognizing her. "You deceived us. You convinced the woman and then she convinced me."

"You used your freedom," said the Serpent. "That is how it had to happen."

"And what do we do now?"

"Live, grow, multiply, die. That is what you were created for, to have knowledge of Good and Evil. If Elokim hadn't wanted you to eat the fruit, he wouldn't have given you freedom. His pride is wounded, nevertheless, that you dared defy him. He will get over it. He is casting you out because he fears that you will eat of the Tree of Life and never die. He wants to hold the power of eternity over you."

"You should have told me that if we also ate *that* fruit we could avoid death," Eve sighed.

The Serpent clicked her tongue. Eve restrained a gesture of repugnance when she saw that it was forked.

"You are incorrigible," the Serpent said. "But do not believe that eternity is a gift. You will have an ephemeral life, but I assure you that you will not be bored. Because you will not have eternal life, you will have to reproduce, and that will keep you occupied. And now I must go, escape before he takes away my gift of speech—something he has done more than once. Go that way. You will find a cave."

The ground was rocking again. Streams of refulgent, thundering light burst against the sky. In the blink of an eye, the Serpent disappeared, agile, and wriggling away through the undergrowth.

Adam looked at the woman. They were holding on to each other, attempting to keep their balance.

Stumbling, they looked for a tree to give them support. They clung to its trunk to keep from falling. Eve's eyes, wide with fright, were darting here and there, not focusing on anything. He smelled her fear, for the first time experiencing uncertainty, the terror of not knowing what to do, where to go. If only the ground would stop moving, he thought. With Eve, he slid down to the ground. He held her tight. Like him, she was trembling, doubled over with her head between her knees. He heard her pleading with the Earth to stop shaking.

CHAPTER 7

*W*HEN THE EARTH STOPPED SHAKING AND THEY WERE able to stand, they peered into the precipice that separated them from Paradise. The splendor that had until then shone above their heads had been replaced by a strange, dull gray sky, a chrome penumbra filled with clouds of dust. They looked into the fissure and through the thick yellow fog tried to make out some way by which they could return to the Garden, but the abyss completely encircled it. Adam knelt, touched his forehead to the loose rock of the edge, and pounded the ground with a fist as he moaned a lament of rage and desperation. Eve stared at him with dismay. She could not explain the catastrophe, or Elokim's violent reaction. Had such fury been provoked by her having dared eat of the fruit or by the knowledge that she and Adam had acquired in the cave? Had he cast them out so he would not have to witness what evolved from them, what she had seen in the waters of the river? When they chose, and opted for what they did not know, had he felt belittled? There was no doubt that the

40

Garden was beautiful—oh, so beautiful!—or that he had made sure that they lacked for nothing.

"I never thought he would cast us out," Eve said aloud.

"What did you think, Eve? What did you think?" Adam asked, turning to look at her, reproaching her.

"I told you. He wanted me to eat of the fruit. He made me feel that was what he wanted. He is curious to know what will come from us. That is why he made us free. At least, that's what I thought."

"And did you think all that would take place in the Garden?"

"I thought the whole earth would be our Garden."

Adam looked at her with pity. "You were mistaken," he said.

"We still don't know what there is farther on, Adam. It may be that we will find what I saw. Elokim must know what he is doing."

The man's smile was ironic and melancholy. What could he expect of her, other than curiosity? She was blessed that this was how she responded to uncertainty. He, on the other hand, felt paralyzed, filled with fear and repentance. He did not want to move from where they were. He clung to the possibility that Elokim would think it over and allow them to return.

"I think that we should ask Elokim to forgive us, prostrate ourselves until he allows us to return."

Eve felt his anxiety on the soles of her feet, on the palms of her hands, and in the misty liquid that had pooled in her eyes and was beginning to trickle down her cheeks. Adam felt the woman's warmth at his back, and the moisture of her tears. Slowly, he rose up and looked once more toward the Garden. It was floating in the distance, in clear, unreal air. From the twisted, leafy branches of the Tree of Life issued the golden, placid radiance that had until then given them light. He wondered whether they would survive without it. Could Elokim be playing a trick on them to make them nostalgic over their loss? Eve left Adam's side and slowly walked to the very edge of the abyss. As the thick smoke dissipated, thinning as it rose, the outlines of the Garden of Eden became more clearly defined. She could see the paths they had walked so often, the plants and trees whose names they knew. She heard the noise of the rivers that now, without beds, spilled noisily over the precipice. She went back to Adam.

"I don't think that Elokim wants to hear us yet," she told him, stroking his hand. "The Earth has only now stopped trembling. We will have to wait until he gets over being angry with us. Why don't we go look and see what is there beyond the place where the sky touches the ground? Look how the dust is beginning to clear. Let's go, Adam. Later we can do what you suggest."

He accepted her arguments with resignation. They began to walk, leaving the garden at their back. Through clear intervals in the dust cloud they saw a wide, rugged plain of red earth carpeted with yellow grass dotted here and there with clumps of palms and cedars. Along one side ran the sharp, jagged peaks of precipitous mountains that seemed to have erupted from the ground. At a distance it was impossible to judge, they saw a rock formation. Enormous plates of stone stood out from it as if extruded from some dark region. Farther on, piled-up rocks formed a strange and solitary mountain. Up this mountain snaked the green that spread along the plain until it was lost at the far limits. This landscape seemed not new but exhausted, fragmented, battered. They were intimidated by its enormity and the arbitrary way in which the rocks, grass, and vegetation were arranged, so unlike the Garden. Could it be Elokim who had laid out all that, Adam wondered, amazed that such a desolate and hostile landscape could exist so near the Garden. Eve walked on, trying to subdue the sensation that she had suddenly grown smaller. She felt minute, fragile. He eyes were burning and her nose felt raw.

"What could it be over there where the sky ends, Adam? Could it be another precipice?"

"That's the horizon," he said. "Look how it is moving as we walk along."

Eva looked at the clouds. Where are they going? she wondered. She had never wondered about that in the Garden when she was stretched out beside the river watching them roll by overhead.

Without discussing it, they turned their steps toward a green blanket of pine trees. Eve stopped from time to time. She picked up rocks from the ground, dried grass. She smelled them. She thought about the Tree of Life and the Tree of Knowledge, so alike and at the same time so different. The land outside the Garden had features and smells that recalled their Paradise, and yet things in this place all seemed to offer contrasting possibilities. The stones, for example, could be hurtful and dig into the soles of their feet, or might simply lie there, presenting their hard, sharp edges for her to look at. Did Good and Evil exist in everything around them? she wondered. She gave a start when she reached out to touch a perfect blue wildflower. It had thorns! She had never imagined that a flower could cause pain.

Adam watched Eve step around the rocks in the path. They had dug into his feet as well, forcing him to hop around them to avoid the stabbing sensation that ran from his legs to his chest. Ever since they had left the Garden, the same body that only a short while ago had provided pleasure had done nothing but cause a myriad of sensations that he could not understand or suppress. The fine dust floating in the air burned his throat; the ashen light that clung to his flesh was choking him and making his skin wet and salty. New words—"pain," "sweat"—emerged in his consciousness and gave a name to his bewildering discomfort. Each time Eve stepped away from him to touch unfamiliar trees, plants, and small flowers, he turned and looked back at the Garden with longing. He wondered anxiously whether Elokim would get past his wrathful impulse to cast them out forever and leave them exposed and alone in this enormous, inhospitable place.

Along the way, Adam saw a falcon. It soared in circles in the distance. Animals, he thought. He had forgotten them. Where were they? What had become of them? The lowering white sky weighed down on him. He wondered if that thin light would be as constant as the warm golden light of the Garden. The sensation of his sweaty skin and the heat that inflamed his body forced him to walk more slowly. Eve was sweating, too. The gleam of her wet skin attracted him. He went to her and ran his hand down her back, along her arms. He noticed how reddish her skin had become, and thought that it might be the reflection of the reddish earth. Although they kept walking, they came no closer to the distant greenness. Eve listened to the wind. Where was it coming from? It was like Elokim, invisible but present. It seemed to her that she heard laughter. She thought that it might be those *others* she had seen. She could not conceive of the possibility that they were alone in such immensity. In the waters of the river she had seen many beings. Again she heard the laughter. She stopped. She signaled to Adam not to speak.

"Do you hear that? Someone is laughing."

"The Serpent. She must be around somewhere."

Adam looked up. They were very near one of the strange rock formations that emerged from the earth like enormous monoliths whose walls showed bands shading from pale rose to orange. The laughter was clearer. It did not sound like the Serpent. Adam ran toward the rocks the sound was coming from. Eve followed. They saw shapes moving at the top of one of the promontories. Hyenas. Six or seven of them. The man smiled. He remembered when that name was forming in his mind to be completed in his mouth. For the first time he associated the sound of the hyenas with his own laughter. He called to them. The animals always came when he called. The hyenas did not obey. They were sniffing the air. Their laughter faded into hoarse grunts. They were watching Adam and Eve and pacing restlessly. Eve saw one of them begin to start down toward them. Without knowing why, she felt a cold shiver down her spine.

"They don't recognize us, Adam," she said, on her guard, as a knot tightened in her chest. "Don't call them anymore. Let's leave."

Adam looked at her oddly. He brushed aside her concern with a gesture that conveyed his dominion over beasts. He called them again.

Eve, frightened, moved back. Now two more hyenas were coming down from the rocks. Those left behind were pacing around above them as if they could not decide what to do, restless, making strange, menacing sounds.

Dismissing Eve's warnings, Adam went to meet them. When he was only a few steps from them, he held out his hand to touch them, as was his habit with any animal in the Garden. Only then did he realize how much they had changed from what they had once been. The boldest hyena crouched and then sprang toward Adam, slashing at him with a paw that raked his hand. That was the signal for the others to come running down from the rocks. Eve screamed as loud as she could, stooped down, picked up a few rocks and threw them with all her strength at the band of animals. Frightened by her scream, surprised by the rocks, the hyenas stopped.

Adam followed Eve's example and began throwing rocks as he retreated.

Stunned by what had happened, possessed by the anguish pounding in their chests, spurred by instinct, the man and woman began to run as fast as they could in the direction of the Garden.

Just as they neared the chasm, Adam, sweating, his face registering his agitation, took Eve by the shoulders.

"We must ask for forgiveness, Eve. We must prostrate ourselves and beg Elokim to let us return. You have to promise me that you will never again eat of the forbidden fruit."

"Never," she said, consenting, ready to do anything to escape

Adam's panicked expression and the fear that was making her knees tremble.

"We still haven't learned all the things Elokim knows. He has no reason to reproach us. We haven't changed."

Eve looked at him. She didn't want to tell him that there was no longer any trace of the radiant splendor his body had once exuded; nor did she mention that he seemed to be growing smaller. She did not want to think about the hissing sound of air entering her lungs. The weight of her fear, the frenetic race to escape the hyenas, was making it difficult for her to breathe. Adam was right. The best course would be to return, to beg, to humble themselves.

They prostrated themselves at the very edge of the deep, open chasm. The air in it was now clear, and at the very bottom they could see rocks with sharp points angled toward them. On the other side, the resplendent foliage of the Tree of Life was visible. Adam avidly gulped air. If he could make a jump that would put him back in the Garden, he would never leave it again, he thought. Still prostrate beside Eve, with his mouth brushing the sandy ground, he shouted out his repentance, every lament and plea he was able to express. Eve seconded him, shamed and contrite, lifting her voice until she felt that all her ardor was consumed in that supplication.

A burst of wind suddenly rose out of the precipice and enveloped them, rumpling their hair and stripping off the leaves they had used to cover their nakedness. Before their eyes the wind became visible, a thin, blazing entity, a gigantic reddish orange blade expanding and contracting, crackling at their feet, hotter and more terrible than any heat they had experienced. The tongue of fire launched itself at them, licking the soles of their feet, the palms of their hands, scorching their skin, flashing out against them. They scrambled to their feet and began to run, away from the precipice. Not relenting an instant, the fire came right behind them, driving them unmercifully across the plain until they reached the mountain in the middle of the rocky formation. With their arms crossed over their heads, protecting themselves as best they could, their feet raw and painful, Adam and Eve reached the side of the mountain and laboriously climbed, followed closely by the flame. In the midst of some thorny bushes, they could see the mouth of a cave. As suddenly as it had appeared, the flame disappeared with a quiet whoosh. They understood that they had come to what would be their dwelling in the hostile land to which they had been exiled. Paralyzed with fright, they sought refuge in each others' arms, shaken by sobbing they could not contain.

"That demonstration of power was almost as impressive as the creation," said the Serpent, who had appeared on a rock nearby. "And to think that all you did was eat the fruit."

"Why didn't I think to eat of the Tree of Life? Why didn't you tell me to do that? Why? Why?" Eve queried between sobs.

"You are misguided if you think that Elokim would have permitted that. Even the freedom he gave you two has its limits."

"Today we were attacked by hyenas," said Adam. "What will happen when other animals do that?"

"You will have to learn to distinguish between those you can trust and those you cannot. The animals are beginning to know the sensation of hunger."

"What is that?" Eve asked.

"Hunger, thirst. You will know them. And you will know what to do. Little by little you will become aware of all you know. You have it inside you. You have only to find it. Go into your cave. Rest. You have had a difficult day."

"Day?"

"Day, night. Arbitrary measurements based on the rotation of the stars. Rest, Eve. Stop asking questions."

CHAPTER 8

T WAS A LARGE CAVE. IRREGULAR FLAT ROCKS PRO-
truded from the walls, leaving a space in the center covered with fine, dark sand. The sides curved upward to close in
a kind of dome pierced at the highest point by an opening that
let in light. After the heat of the fire and the brightness of the
day, the cool and dark were a relief.

Eve dropped down upon a flat stone. Adam looked at his
wife's back. Her long legs tucked up against her chest. She
looked like the petal of a flower. Despite the prediction that
they would die on the day they ate of the Tree, he continued
to feel just as intensely aware of his body and as alive as he had
since he first tried the fruit. Only his fear of another unexpected and cruel punishment prevented him from entering the
woman again and waiting inside her for the agitation and woe
that engulfed him to calm. Eve began to beseech him to teach
her how to distinguish life from death, and he did not know
how to do it without touching her. So many new and painful

sensations crammed so close together scarcely allowed him to think.

"I have never felt this pain I have in my feet, on my skin. My mouth is filled with sand; my throat burns. Don't you think this is death?" Eve moaned, inconsolable.

"Death is the opposite of life," Adam said. "You are feeling all this because you are alive. This is what you wanted, Eve, isn't that true?" he heard himself say despite himself, as he sat down beside her. "You wanted knowledge. This is knowledge: good and evil, pleasure and pain, Elokim and the Serpent, each image has is opposite reflection."

It's because of her that I know I am alive, he thought. Although their bodies no longer radiated light, although they were diminished in size and the delicate tail that had formerly protected their hidden orifices had disappeared, the desire to touch her prevented him from confusing death with the anguish of profound abandonment. Eve listened. However often she wiped her eyes, they filled with water again and again. She was unable to regain her tranquillity, or calm her hands, her feet, her mouth. Her pain flowed into words. The scratches, cuts, burns. Perhaps Adam's body was stouter. Or perhaps the pain hadn't penetrated and contaminated his thoughts. She felt that the heat from the wounds in her skin had leaped to the hollow space inside her, a precipice equal to the one that separated them from the Garden. Elokim's cruelty and what was happening to them had squeezed the life out of her, leaving her with no spirit, no energy to understand why what she had done deserved the whiplash of fire that had driven them here.

"I'm thirsty," she said. "Thirst is what the thing that has left our mouths so dry is called. Help me look for water. Water satiates thirst."

She could barely speak. She had an unbearable burning in her throat, a grainy dryness on her teeth.

Adam explored the cave. He had heard the faint sound of water when he entered. Toward the back he found a tiny spring that threaded down one of the walls and ran along a narrow channel to empty into the hollow of a rock. They took turns dipping their heads and faces into it, opening their lips and washing the sand from their teeth. The water soothed their parched mouths. They filled their cheeks but did not dare swallow the water. It was cold, the opposite of fire, but it burned just as much. They both spat at the same moment. They were afraid that the water would burst open their chests.

On a rock they found long pieces of a strange substance covered with hair, like that on the skin of sheep. They covered themselves with it, tying it around the waist. The hair was soft and lustrous. Slowly they began to warm. They lay down on the rock. Adam watched Eve's eyes close. He lay down beside her, put his arms around her, and his eyes, too, closed.

Eve awakened. She did not want to wake completely because she had dreamed she was back in the Garden and her consciousness still did not clearly distinguish between reality and imagination, but curiosity to know whether or not the terrible things she remembered had happened opened her eyes. She saw nothing. She opened them as wide as she could, and still could not see. She thought about crows. The color of their wings inundated everything. She held out her hands to touch the dense darkness. She sat straight up. Her fingers closed on black, blind air. Her eyes were no longer useful. She touched her face to be sure she was awake. She fumbled with her hands, with rising panic.

"Adam. Adam! *Adam!*" she shouted. She felt him move, wake, groan. Then a long silence and a yell. "Where are you, Eve? Where are you?"

"Can't you see me?"

"No. I don't see anything. Everything is black."

"I think we're dead," she moaned. "What else could this be?"

She groped around her until she touched him. He felt her cold fingers. He could not understand that she had disappeared. He could not see her. A croaking sound escaped his throat.

"I don't like death, Eve. Get me out of this."

Within them, as in the first time of Paradise, they heard the voice. It sounded both ironic and gentle.

"It is night," the voice said. "I made it so you would rest, for now you will have to work to survive. At night you will sleep. You will have no volition. That way you will be able to enter your consciousness. Simultaneously know it and forget it."

Eve perceived that communication with the voice was open for her. She was not afraid.

"You are cruel," she said.

"You disobeyed."

"Don't tell me that you didn't plan this. You did not conceive us to be eternal. You knew as well as I that this would happen."

"Of course. But that was my challenge. Not to intervene. To allow you your freedom."

"And to punish us."

"It is too early to make that judgment. I admit that I always knew what would happen. But it had to be this way."

"Give us back the light."

"Go later with Adam to the cave entrance. The light will be there, waiting for you. Day after day. From now on you will exist in time."

"At least we're not dead," Eve sighed when the voice stilled.

At dawn, Adam watched as the shadows lifted and dispersed like mist. Eve was sleeping. Was she perhaps looking inside her consciousness? Where was it one went when sleeping? Did she understand what to him was incomprehensible? He didn't like to see her asleep, or to sleep himself. He didn't like it when his eyes closed and his mind no longer belonged to him. And yet, in the darkness of the cave it had been a relief to abandon himself to that strange immobility, to listen to the cry of his body to lie quietly and cease to feel pain and nostalgia, fear and uncertainty. Suddenly his anxiety returned. Had Elokim carried out his promise to bring back the light?

He walked to the cave entrance, and what he saw frightened him so badly he could not contain a cry. The whitish sky of the previous day was now blazing from end to end; even the clouds were on fire. He called Eve. She came quickly, moving unsteadily, as if she had only recently learned to walk. She looked at the red sky. She stepped past him and went outside, holding out her arms to the warm air. On the sky she saw the red circle of the sun rising from the horizon.

"The sky is in flames, but the fire will not reach the Earth," she said.

Adam went to her. His eyes were filled with tears.

Eve nestled against his chest. He, who was taller, rested his head on hers and broke into sobs. What would they do? he asked. How could they exist so far from the Garden now that their bodies ached and they were thirsty? What have we done, Eve? What have we done? What use is knowledge to us in the midst of this desolation? Look at the vastness around us. What will we do? Where will we go?

Eve did not know what to answer. Nothing was as she had imagined. She put her arms around Adam. She did not want to see him suffer. His sorrow resonated inside her, gave her shivers. She wanted to wrap herself around him, grow more hands to caress him. The impatience he often provoked in her dissipated. In its place she felt a wish to console him and love him that was both strong as the wind and as gentle and singing as the murmur of water in the river. She wondered whether his skin could perceive what she felt, if he could smell it, if knowing her tenderness for him would calm his worries.

"Let's try death, Eve," said Adam, suddenly standing upright. "Maybe if we die we can return to the Garden."

"You just said that you don't like death."

"I thought that the night was death. Perhaps it is not knowing what it is that frightens us."

"And how will we manage to die? It won't be easy," said Eve, bewildered.

"I have an idea. Let's climb to the top of this mountain," he said, pulling himself together, animated by his resolve.

He started up the mountain. She followed, reluctantly. She didn't know what it was to die. The Serpent had said that death was feeling nothing, but no explanation had been given about what followed. Maybe it was worth a try. Maybe the best way to bring an end to their doubts was to find out whether death was really so terrible. Better to know than to suffer the uncertainty of ignorance.

The mountain rose high above the cave. Great stones protruded here and there, and among them the ground was sandy and dotted with thorny bushes. As they climbed, their bodies felt heavier. Their feet, the palms of their hands burned against the rough sand. The sky had changed. It was blue now. With no clouds. The fire had been extinguished and the disk of the sun shone with an intense white light impossible to look into. Again they felt intense heat lacerating their skin. Eve's feet were bleeding. I can't go any farther, she said. You go on alone, but Adam picked her up, threw her over his shoulder, and kept plodding on, panting, sweating, completely drained. He could not comprehend his fatigue, how laborious it was to do what previously had cost no effort. Eve moaned, whimpered. Her laments crept into his nostrils, his eyes, his ears, and tore at him inside. Silently, he cursed Elokim. At last they reached the top. They could view endless land, smoking volcanoes, the island of the Garden of Eden, rivers running toward the sea.

Eve said nothing. Although it was different from Paradise, the landscape was beautiful. Beautiful and strangely hers.

"If we die now, we will never see all this again," she said.

"I went with you to eat the fruit," said Adam. "You come with me now."

After a wordless and fleeting moment of doubt and lamentation, Adam leaped from the promontory into the void. Eve jumped after him.

They fell headlong, air whistling in their ears. Eve closed her eyes, clamped her lips shut.

Adam watched as the red dust of the ground stirred and rolled into a dizzily whirling wind tunnel that enveloped them, broke their fall, then transported them through the air and gently dropped them into a current of water.

Again the voice spoke within them.

"This is not the time to die," it told them. "You will know death at its proper moment. And when it comes, you will wish for it to hold off a little longer."

CHAPTER 9

S HIVERING, THEY SWAM TILL THEY EMERGED FROM the water. They recognized the palms, cedars, and pines, the banks of the river they had seen from a distance. So this was where Elokim had carried them. On the grass they found more dry skins to clothe themselves. The sun shone high in the sky. They lay on the riverbank, not speaking, confused but wiser from the experience. Little by little, warmth enveloped their bodies and calmed the trembling caused by vertigo and the fearful fall.

"I was terrified," said Eve. "Don't ask me again to give death a try."

Adam nodded. He had swallowed a lot of water. The crystalline liquid was good; it cooled his throat, his mouth. Cautiously, he waited a while to be sure that nothing bad had happened to him, and then urged Eve to drink.

"Drink, Eve, drink. Nothing will happen to you. It tastes very good," he said, taking her hand and helping her bend down from a rock to take the water in the hollow of a hand and bring it to her lips.

Eve drank. She sipped the liquid with pleasure, sucking the last drop from her fingers and dipping in again and again. Adam smiled. He admired how she never did anything halfway. Whether she did it out of trust or defiance, he wasn't sure. But this time her face unequivocally signaled pleasure.

"See how Elokim saved you when you had decided to die! Who can understand him! I told you he was erratic. He acts one way and then regrets it. One thing is for sure: he is very curious to see what you will do with the freedom you took."

They looked up. The Serpent was coiled around the branch of a shrub whose trunk leaned out over the river.

"You again," said Adam.

"I've been alone, too. I'm bored."

"If we had died, would we have gone back to Paradise?" Eve asked. "Is that why he saved us, to prevent us from returning?"

"From death there is no returning. Better not to try that again. You haven't lived long enough. It is life that will bring you closer to Paradise."

"Tell us how," said Adam.

"I can't help you. Elokim no longer confides in me. I am alone."

"But you know a lot."

"Knowledge is not the solution to everything. You will discover that as you go along. I'm leaving. I'm tired of answering so many questions."

She slipped agilely through the tree branches and disappeared.

Eve lay back on the grass, pensive. Adam lay beside her.

For a long time they said nothing, staring at the blue, concave sky through the leaves of the trees.

"I wonder if perhaps the Serpent is Elokim's Eve," she said. "When we were in the Garden she told me she watched him create and forget constellation after constellation. They have known each other a long time."

"Maybe she was inside him the way that you were in me."

"Why do you think Elokim separated us?"

"He thought that we could exist as a single body, but it didn't work out. You were in too deep. You couldn't see or hear. That is why he decided to separate us, to take you out of me. That is why it feels so good when the two of us are one again."

"But you still believe that I am responsible for everything that's happened because I gave you fruit from the Tree of Knowledge. You could have refused to eat it."

"True. But once you had eaten it, I had to eat. I thought you would cease to exist. I didn't want to be left alone. If I hadn't eaten of the fruit and the Other had banished you from the Garden, I would have left to look for you."

Eve's eyes filled with water.

"I never doubted that you would eat," she said.

"And that day I saw you as if I had never known you till then. Your skin was gleaming, all soft and shining. And you looked at me as if suddenly you remembered the exact place you existed inside me before the Other separated us."

"Your legs impressed me. And your chest. So broad. Yes, I did want to be inside you again. I see you in my dreams. You have a body like a tree. You protect me so the sun won't burn me."

As one, they got up together and went back into the water to cool off.

"Euphrates," said Adam. "That's the name of this river."

They floated in the current, abandoning themselves to the sensation of the crystalline liquid. It was not difficult to understand the joy of the fishes whose colors they had often admired. Adam opened his lips and slowly sipped the cool fluid. He thought about the taste of the forbidden fruit and reached for Eve. They kissed as one entered the other, astounded at the amazing sensations they received from their light, slippery bodies. For a long while they were quiet, tightly embraced, each attempting to recover the lost memory of being a single creature, to grasp the images each of them guarded inside and pour into those the river of their own. Unsuccessfully, they traveled the dim passageways of their minds, wanting to penetrate the other's sensations but unable to transcend the space where each of them existed irreparably alone within the limits of their bodies. As much as they tried, they could not glimpse the intricate landscape in which their most intimate thoughts dwelled. It was recognition of this impenetrable barrier that finally enveloped them and caused their muscles and bones to open without misgivings and engage in only intimacy fully conceded to them, the one they reached on the riverbank, amid the mud and algae on the shore.

When they started walking back to the cave, the splendor of the day gave way to the soft, welcoming, light of evening. A breeze was blowing. They left behind the trees on the riverbank and cut through open field toward the mountain. On the way they sighted in the distance a group of elephants and a herd of long-horned oryx. The oryx seemed, like them, to be disoriented, just wandering. They too had eaten the forbidden fruit, she thought. Maybe they held Adam and her responsible for being expelled from the Garden. Adam remembered the hyenas. He wondered whether these oryx would be docile or would attack them. Eve suggested that they not go too close.

"I miss Cain," said Adam, remembering the faithful dog who had been his companion in the Garden.

"And I the cat," said Eve. "Come, let's go to the Garden and look for them."

CHAPTER 10

*W*HEN THEY WERE AGAIN WITHIN SIGHT OF THE precipice and the distant mystery of the enclosed Garden, Adam surrendered once more to the weakness of tears. If he had been an animal, he would have howled with pain as he stood before that mirage whose inexplicable beauty was a constant flame in his memory. Internally he struggled to silence his reproaches against the woman, the Serpent, and Elokim. It did little good to rationalize, or to talk with her; in his innermost being he could not ease the weight of having been dislodged from that place where he had been created to exist as the most special and happy of creatures.

He watched Eve walk along, occasionally stopping at some flowering bushes to smell the blossoms. He noticed that her skin was darker, golden, as if somehow she had managed to preserve the glow of Paradise. He caught up with her. They should not go too close to the precipice, he said. They didn't want the fire to lash out at them again and force them to retreat.

They walked to a prudent distance from the abyss, one toward the east and the other toward the west. The plants that during the cataclysm had been torn from the fertile soil of the Garden were taking root in the red earth, refusing to perish. As they went, they encountered in their path high grasses, brush, plants with saw-toothed, spiny leaves that tore at their legs, making it difficult for them to pass. They learned the poison of the ants and the bite of gnats and mosquitoes. Eve talked to the insects, telling them to obey and leave her and Adam in peace. After realizing that this had no effect, Adam just kept going, swiping right and left. They saw rabbits, pheasants, squirrels, and mice that instead of approaching when they called fled in fear. In the distance, Adam heard the howling of wolves and pictured them cringing, far away. He wondered if the ones he had encountered might have met others like them, already experienced in living outside the confines of the Garden. He missed the lions with their golden manes, the giraffe with its long neck and sweet eyes, the magnificent phoenix, and, of course, his strong, clever dog, always obedient to his wishes.

"Cain," he called. "Cain."

Late that afternoon, he found Cain. The dog was playing with a coyote, unaware of the man who was looking for him. When he saw Adam, Cain pricked up his ears and ran up to lick the man's hands. Adam knelt down and hugged him. The man was as happy as the dog when he knew he was recognized. The coyote observed them for a moment. It seemed to be about to join in their games, but instead it turned and disappeared into the brush. Eve smiled when she saw the man rolling on the ground with Cain. She and the cat had never played like that. The cat never treated her like another cat; in contrast, Cain was jumping and playing as if Adam were another dog.

It wasn't easy for Eve when finally she found the cat. She called to it with sweet words, trying to persuade it to come down from the tree where it was crouched, skittish and mewing pitiably. Eve spat into her hand to offer it liquid for its dry mouth. The animal came to her very slowly, moving deliberately along a low branch, but after she scratched its back, it came down out of the tree and rubbed against her legs.

Accompanied by the dog and the cat, the man and woman started back toward the cave. Adam went first. He would throw a piece of wood and the dog would pick it up and come running back to give it to him. Adam was smiling. Eve had not seen him smile since the fire had driven them from the Garden. He was moving along confidently, sure he was on the right course. She admired his sense of direction. He didn't use his nose like the dog. He held out an arm, looked along it, frowned, and seemed to know which way to go. His back was very broad. Maybe that was what gave him better orientation. The landscape confused her. The plain was so vast. She looked at the cat, trotting at her side with its light steps. Although they didn't speak, the animals were a comfort against the abandonment and the solitude. They disappeared at times into the undergrowth, but came when they were called.

They walked a long time. Eve's body felt heavier and heavier, and the hollow that since morning had been growling in her stomach began to hurt. She imagined a small animal scratching inside her, chewing on her. She had never felt anything like that. She looked at Adam out of the corner of her eye; he, too, was walking slowly. The sky was changing color, filling with clouds whose rims had turned magenta and pink. She heard a kind of bellow. She turned. Adam was doubled over, clutching his stomach.

"Do you feel hollow inside? Does it hurt?"

"This is hunger, Eve."

"What shall we do?"

"I don't know."

"The cave is still some distance away. Mine hurts, too. I don't want to walk any farther."

"Let's look for a tree. We'll sit down."

They looked for a tree they could rest against. They had to walk quite a way to find one. On the plain, trees were sparse, small. The palm trees, on the other hand, went straight up, slim, with long branches scurrying from the wind. Finally they found a comfortable position on the ground. The dog and cat curled up beside them. Hunger, like fatigue, had arrived suddenly. Lethargic, Adam fell asleep. Eve watched day turning into evening. The darkness seemed soft this time, a dense fog enveloping everything. After a while her eyes could make out the silhouettes of everything near them. That soothed her. She heard whistling, the cries of sad birds, harsh and indescribable sounds. She observed that the darkness of the sky was sprinkled with holes that let light through. She wondered if it was through them that the white petals, which had once been their food, had fallen. This memory, combined with the one of forbidden figs she had tasted, thickened her saliva and cramped her stomach. Adam remembered he had heard the voice condemning them to grasses and thorns. Eve patted the earth around her, pulled some blades of grass, chewed them. The bland, slightly bitter taste depressed her. She regretted eating the fruit, acting so sure of herself, so defiant in the Garden. She wondered if everything she had so longed to know would turn out to be worth the pain. Knowledge and freedom were of so little use in quieting hunger, she thought. If she had been more docile, would Elokim have left them in the Garden? Why had he acted so offended if it was all part of his plan? Perhaps Elokim confused the worlds he had created and forgot the designs he imposed on them. She had to be ingenuous to think that when she ate of the fruit the perverse or adventurous sense of all this would be revealed to her.

Adam woke beneath the red sky of dawn. This time it did not cause him anguish, it enlivened him. He decided that he preferred day to night. A few steps from the tree they had taken shelter beneath, he saw other trees, with green fruit. He left Eve sleeping and went to one tree. He touched a fruit, then picked it. Pears, he thought. His mouth filled with saliva. He gave one to the dog. He watched him bite it. He saw the juice of the fruit dripping from its jaws. He pulled off another. He did not complete the move to put it in his mouth. He threw it as far away as he could. The dog ran after it. Adam buried his face in his hands. He smelled the fragrance of the pear on his fingers. No! he exclaimed, overwhelmed by a sudden fear that was stronger than hunger. The scent of the fruit had left him dazed. He could not take the risk, he told himself. If Elokim became enraged again, Adam did not even want to imagine what punishment he would impose on them this time. Fruit was dangerous. Its flesh was filled with Elokim's rage. If they ate fruit, he would cast them even farther away. They would never be able to return to the Garden.

He woke Eve. She smelled the aroma of the pear on his hands.

"What is that smell, Adam? Have you eaten?"

He showed her the pear. But he hadn't eaten it, he said. Neither he nor she should eat the pears.

Eve jumped up. She ran to the tree. He followed.

"He forbade us to eat the fruit from a certain tree, Adam, not all trees."

"He forbade us to eat of one tree and he cast us out of the Garden so we would not eat of the other. I tell you, we must not eat fruits. They are dangerous. We *cannot* take that risk again, Eve."

Incredulous, she stared at him. Hunger was gnawing at her innards. The fragrance of the pears so tantalizingly near made it impossible for her to think. She reached out to take one. Adam stopped her. The dog began to bark.

"You can't force me not to eat."

"Look at us, Eve, alone, hungry, abandoned. What other disastrous move of yours do you want me to share?"

Eve felt her face and chest burn. Filled with rage and frustration, she contained her desire to throw herself on Adam. The strength of that reaction frightened her. Shamed, confused, she started running. She ran and ran. In the light, cool morning breeze she regained her calm. Adam ran after her. "Where are you going? Why are you running?" he shouted.

She stopped.

"It makes me furious that every time you want me to obey you, you remind me that I ate the fruit."

"When I lose hope I can't help it," he said.

"Eating it was your decision."

"Yes, but it was you who offered the fruit to me. You ate first."

"I didn't know what would happen. You didn't know either."

"We knew that we might die."

"That wasn't what happened."

"It didn't happen at that instant, but we will die."

"You've seen that Elokim didn't let us die. Don't you believe that our coming to know each other was worth the grief? And the taste of the fig? And the cool of the water?"

"And hunger? And pain?"

"We wouldn't be hungry if you would stop being afraid."

They started back toward the mountain that held their cave. A shadow was circling over their heads. Adam looked up. After an instant's blindness from looking toward the sun, he saw against the light blue of afternoon the sumptuous plumage of his favorite bird, its immense orange and gold wings, the small head crowned by an intense blue panache. It was the Phoenix.

"The Phoenix was the only one of the animals that didn't eat from the Tree of Knowledge," exclaimed Eve. "I'm sure that it goes in and out of the Garden without being stopped by the fire."

Adam wondered if it could be a sign. Perhaps the Phoenix would carry them back to the Garden, flying over the precipice. With that possibility he was swamped by a wave of laughter and levity. He wanted to jump up and down, wave his arms. On one occasion before the woman arrived, the bird had carried him to the sea. It had set him down on the water, and Adam had seen the languid, buoyant creatures that dwelled there. He named the swordfish, the whale, the shark, the manta rays and dolphins, the schools of sardines, the seashells and starfish. He had observed the warm abysses and the mouths that served as vents for vapor from suboceanic fires. Luminous fish had accompanied him on an exploration, and for the first time he had intuited darkness. It was this intuition of a world without light that his memory had evoked during the first night of darkness in his lifetime. He was remembering the small, colorful fish he associated with Eve's toes just when the bird descended, stirring a placid breeze and depositing two figs before her. Then it took off, directing its beak and its wings toward the Garden of Eden.

Eve picked up the figs. Just seeing them filled her mouth with the anticipated flavor of the juice and the flesh of the fruit. Quick as the cat, Adam took them from her hands.

"No, Eve, I told you no fruits. Most of all, figs."

He clutched the figs in his hands. His eyes followed the course of the Phoenix. As he watched it leave without carrying them back to the Garden, he was paralyzed with disappointment.

"I am really, really hungry," said Eve, frightened. "We must eat, Adam. We have to eat."

"I am as hungry as you, but our misfortune gives me pause."

"But the bird brought these, Adam. The Other must have sent them."

"We don't know that, Eve. I thought that the Phoenix would carry us back. But these figs—we don't know, Eve, if this is another trick," he said stubbornly. "We still don't know if the Other is for us or against us."

Silenced by Adam's blindness and stubbornness, Eve swallowed her tears, tasting the salt in her dry mouth.

"Please, Adam. Don't throw away the figs. Keep them."

Adam buried them at the entrance to the cave. He dug the earth with the help of a sharp rock. Under the starry night, Eve persisted in her attempts to make him stop. There are two, Adam. Give me one. She did not persuade him. They lay down to sleep without speaking, without touching, each thinking of the other's harsh judgment. Her hunger made her picture the fig deteriorating in the earth, food that could be in her mouth lost through the man's intransigence, his cruelty. He was cruel when he forced her to watch as he buried the fruit; more so because he had decided for both of them. He had acted as if her words had no weight, no sound, as if he didn't hear them. And she and her words were one. Not to hear her was to make her nonexistent, to leave her completely alone.

He was aware that he hadn't listened to her. Listening to her made him weak, muddled his intentions. She had too much confidence in herself, and he no longer knew in what, or in whom, to have faith. On the other hand, he knew that he needed her. He missed her warmth, her body.

She was awakened by his hand seeking a refuge. Timidly, he touched her side, hoping she would grant him some way by which he could ease his hand beneath her and enfold her in his arms. At night, Adam always hugged her to him, her back against his chest. Feeling the man searching for her in the darkness aroused her tenderness. The memory of her rage was not enough to make her push him away. She let Adam's arm rest across her breast and pressed close to him. She was cold. The cave was cool and protecting by day, but at night it lost its soul. They had to produce their own heat, snuggling against each other. Silently, she settled into his arms. He whispered into her ear that the next day he would take her to the sea.

CHAPTER 11

*T*HEY WALKED UNTIL THE GULLS AND THE SMELL OF salt came to meet them. Before their eyes appeared an enormous, transparent blue bowl. The dog dashed into the water, unafraid. He leaped about, barking madly. The cat, indifferent, lay down on the sand to contemplate the sea. Adam told Eve about his explorations. He wanted to take her to see what he had seen. They walked into the water. She advanced with caution. The effort it took to push her way through the liquid made her feel limited, clumsy.

"Now, Eve," said Adam, when the water was up to their chins. "Now, sink down, spread your arms and push toward the bottom."

It was useless. However much she tried. She was stymied by the choking in her nose, her mouth, her throat, and the water pushed her back to the surface. Moving her arms and her legs, desperate, she tried to head back toward the beach. She was aware that Adam was following her, confused and embarrassed. "This isn't how it was before," he told her. His body wasn't responding; it wouldn't go any farther down than the depth of a few arm strokes before water entered his every orifice and he couldn't breathe. The sea was to look at, Eve told him when they had reached dry land and had recovered from the salt water they'd swallowed and the battering and bumping the attempt had dealt them, especially Adam. He had been so emphatic in describing the underwater world. Now he doubted he had ever seen it, and wondered if it too was a dream, as much of his life seemed of late.

"But the sea is not only to be looked at," he said with certainty.

Eve lay on the beach and closed her eyes. The sound of the waves regularly slapping on the shore was like the noise of the incessant string of questions forming and dissolving in her mind.

A short while later, Adam returned. He sat down beside her.

"Look, I've brought something for your hunger," he said.

She looked. It was some rough, oval shells. When they were opened, she saw they were filled with a thick, white, trembly substance that left her mouth clean, as if the water had been turned into delicate, briny meat. Adam had laid one on a rock and hammered it with a stone until it revealed the fruit inside. Oysters, he said. Oysters, she repeated, laughing.

"How did you find out that they had something inside we could eat?"

"The same way I knew their name. The same."

They did not go back to the cave until the next day. They spent the night on the beach, some distance apart, humiliated by the uproar in their guts: the noises, the smells, the waste they expelled. At dawn, nauseated, they washed in the ocean. They discussed the possibility that their bodies might have grown rotten, if this was a new punishment for again having put something in their mouths. But then they saw the dog and cat urinate, defecate, and scratch sand over their waste.

"Adam, do you think the animals know they're animals?"

"At least they don't think they may be something different. They don't get confused the way we do."

"Besides animals, what do you think we are?"

"Adam and Eve."

"That isn't an answer."

"Eve, Eve, you never tire of asking questions."

"If it occurs to me to ask it's because there are answers. And we should know them. We ate the fruit, we lost the Garden, and we know almost nothing more than we did before."

They were talking as they returned to the cave. It was doubtless a punishment to think that the body would choose that way to wreak vengeance when they ate, Adam said, but the truth was that he, at least, felt better, with more strength in his muscles, and more spirit.

"It's reasonable. Expelling something that smells so bad makes you lighter. And what a curious sensation—very different from pain, don't you think?"

Smiling, Eve concealed how embarrassed the subject made her feel. To see herself reduced to ingesting and eliminating like the dog and the cat nauseated her, made her feel diminished. She could not understand how Adam seemed to draw something good from what to her was humiliation. She could not understand how he failed to perceive the implicit animality of the experience.

"The Other wasn't playing when he said that dust we are and to dust we will return. These bodies of ours—how long do you think they will last? Adam asked.

"I don't know. I know only that mine hurts more than yours."

Water began to fall from the leaden sky. Large drops beat down on their shoulders. They went running into the cave. The rain was falling in torrents. In the sky, a tree with illuminated, gleaming branches lashed the firmament. The earth answered the assault of the lighted branches with harsh rumblings. In the darkness they saw the sparkling eyes of the cat. The dog sniffed the ground. The four grouped together on the projecting rock that served them as a bed. Embraced, Adam and Eve watched the explosions, the thunder and lightning, astonished and fearful.

"Is the sky going to fall? Are the stars dropping from the sky?" Eve asked.

"I don't think so," said Adam. "They're very far away."

"How do you know?"

"I'm not sure."

Eve awoke bleeding from between her legs. She was terrified when she got to her feet and saw the red liquid flowing from her sex. In the splendor of the dawn, the cave was filled with mist. Even the clouds had taken refuge from the sky's fury, she thought. In her lower abdomen a fist was opening and closing, mortifying her. The red liquid was warm and sticky. The dog came over to her and smelled her. She pushed it away, uneasy. She went to the spring in the cave and washed off, but the blood kept flowing. She woke Adam. He said he would bring her leaves so she could clean off. He told her she should lie down again. They were frightened but they hid their fear from each other. Adam quickly returned. His hands were full of figs and fig leaves, and his face was glowing. With the rain, two figs trees had burst up from the fruit he had buried at the entrance to the cave. The trees, fully grown, were covered with figs.

"Look, Eve, look. You were right. They are for us. We can eat them."

With the leaves and water from the spring, Adam made a poultice for Eve's wound.

"Do you think I'm going to die, Adam? I don't feel as if I'm going to die. I only hurt occasionally."

"It's best if you keep quiet. Eat a fig."

Adam went out with the dog. Lying in the shadows of the cave, Eve opened a fig and scrutinized the sweet, pink interior, the flesh, and the tiny red seeds in the center. My body is different from the man's, she thought. The liquid that comes from him when he is above me, shouting and groaning, is white. Mine is red, and comes out when I am sad. She drew her legs up to her chest. She could not forget his words, blaming her for their misfortunes. The words had hurt as much as the rocks that had torn their feet when they climbed the mountain to jump to the death from which Elokim had rescued them. She was convinced that the reason he had rescued them was the same he had for provoking them to eat of the fruit of the Tree of Knowledge: He wanted to see how they would like being on their own. She had facilitated that for him, though Adam chose not to comprehend. It was easier to blame her than the Other who never allowed himself to be seen.

After the sun set, they were amazed by the brightness of

the night. From the cave, the branches of the fig trees were clearly outlined in an ashen light. They thought that the night was filled with water, and went outside to look. From one side of the celestial dome to the other, the limpid night that followed the rain reminded them of the surface of the sea. High above them hung a round, luminous, pale star, soft and smiling.

"The extinguished sun is beautiful," said Adam.

"It isn't the sun. It's the moon. That is why I'm bleeding."

"How do you know?"

"I know," Eve continued. "I know that inside me there is a sea that the moon fills and empties."

Adam did not ask further. The enchantment of the mystery contained in Eve's unusual tameness, the fragrance of the clear air, the cool light delineating the shapes of the rocks and trees, and the sky rising to infinite heights, sank into his eyes and his skin. Along with his sense of being very small—a vulnerable, lost, and banished creature—he experienced the certainty that he and Eve were an essential part of that desolate nocturnal landscape.

"Do you think we're alone, Eve? Do you think that in this immensity there are no others like you and me?"

"There are others. We have seen them in dreams."

"Could they be hiding inside us? Will they appear while we sleep?"

"I don't know, Adam."

Knowledge, Eve thought, was not the light she had imagined would suddenly suffuse her mind but a slow revelation, a succession of dreams and intuitions that accumulated in a place that predated words; it was the quiet intimacy that was growing between her and her body. In that flowing, in the weight of her lower abdomen and her breasts, in the pain that now filled the place where the man sank himself into her, she sensed a bubbling of life, a spring that would burst from her and flow in every direction. She did not want to leave the cave while she bled. Doubled up, she spent those days dozing, as if dreams were the only reality that interested her.

CHAPTER 12

IGS, PEARS, BITTER FRUITS, GRASSES WITH GOLDEN grains that satisfied the need to chew something, Adam collected everything he thought might drive away hunger, but the hunger returned. Every morning when he opened his eyes he felt it, lodged in the center of his body, living in him like a creature independent of his will, imperious and cruel. What could he give it? the man wondered. Fruit barely placated it, despite the fact that both he and the woman savored the soft pulp and never ceased to be amazed at the ability of the trees to sprout edible things from their branches and leaves. On their walks around the vicinity of the cave, Adam had also tried ants and other insects, and thick, fleshy plants with mysteriously watery interiors. He followed the squirrels and tasted the hard seeds they bit into with their long teeth, but his hunger was greater than all the little things he found and shared with Eve. She, unlike him, never tired of going to the fig tree to satisfy her hunger. She thought that the appearance of the Phoenix carrying the figs in its claws and the way that the trees had grown overnight were an unequivocal signal that those fruits were meant to take the place of the white petals that had been their food in the Garden.

Crouched amid the grasses, fearful of another encounter like the one he'd had with the hyenas, Adam did not dare go too near large animals. Following the cataclysm, there had been many days when he and the woman scarcely noted their presence. Swaying from time to time, the earth lay before them, desolate and silent. Slowly, however, a mixture of sounds—some familiar, others indecipherable—traveled to them through the air. At night they heard the howling of wolves and coyotes, and in the daytime, from far away, came the roar of lions and the powerful trumpeting of elephants. Small animals, pheasants, monkeys, moles, badgers, and rabbits moved through the tall grasses and sometimes they could get close enough to meet their eyes before they scampered away, disappearing into the vegetation, seemingly possessed by the fear that the hyenas inspired in them. Flocks of storks, herons, and ducks flew by overhead. Eve said that their calls touched her heart because they seemed filled with questions.

The cat and the dog intrigued Adam. They ate very little fruit, and yet they did not seem to suffer the pangs of hunger that were mortifying him. What did they do during the long periods they absented themselves from the cave?

He discovered the answer one morning at dawn. He was awakened by a flock of chattering birds that had settled in the branches of the fig trees. He sat on a rock to watch the blackbirds hop about, sing, and peck at the figs. Agitated, the cat meowed and the dog barked without interruption as they circled beneath the trees. Cain pushed up on his hind legs as if he wanted to fly. Arching its back, the cat sloughed off its drowsiness and, with an indecipherable expression, focused on the birds. Suddenly, after clawing the trunk of a tree, the cat stretched and gave an agile leap onto a low branch. It climbed toward the top of the tree and crouched among the leaves. Adam watched, fascinated. He saw how with a swift slash of its paw the cat hooked one of the little birds and clamped its teeth onto the bird's neck. Growling fiercely, using its long claws to stave off the dog, the cat descended the tree and ran to hide in some tall grass. Adam tiptoed over to see what it was doing. He watched it begin its unequal game with the bird, corralling it, clawing it, biting it until it was dead. Then he watched as the cat sank its teeth into the flesh and circumspectly ate it. Revolted, Adam left. Shortly afterward, the cat emerged from its hiding place, cleaned its face, and lay down in the sun for a siesta, well satisfied.

Hunger attacked Adam as suddenly as the repugnance had done. He stood where he was. He took a fig. He bit into it. He wondered if the blood of the bird had a different taste. Suddenly he understood the meaning of the bones and the smells he had noticed in his explorations, the strange laments, the sounds of hidden tigers. He looked at the fig tree with resentment, stomach rumbling. He spit out the fruit. He thought about the long journey to the sea, and the oysters. He knew what he had to do.

He went inside the cave to look for the long pole whose tip he had sharpened with a rock to help in breaking open nuts and digging up bitter roots. "Where are you going?" Eve asked. Adam said that he was going to investigate the sounds of a herd of animals roaming the plain. He wanted to know if they would allow him to come near. He could not explain to himself why he had avoided telling her the truth. "Be careful," she said.

"I will." He left with the dog. The cat stayed with Eve.

The sun was warm in a cloudless sky. Adam decided to go in the direction away from the Garden, toward the open plain beyond which more rock formations and groups of palm trees were visible. If other animals were looking for a way to feed themselves, he could not be sure that they would not consider him food. He was afraid, but he was also driven by urgency. Cain, too, was restless, as if he understood the man's mission.

They had not walked very far when Cain pricked up his ears. Adam saw the rabbit and stooped low. He tried to call the rabbit so it would come of its own accord. "Here, rabbit, rabbit." The little animal sat up on its hindquarters and set its ears straight. The dog ran after it. By the time Adam caught up, the rabbit was already lifeless. Cain was holding it down with a paw and was tearing off pieces with his teeth. Adam stepped back. He let the dog eat. He watched what he was eating, what he left, the uneventful, completely natural way the dog was dealing with its prey, and also the earnestness with which Cain protected his catch even from Adam. When he started toward the dog, it had bared its teeth, growled. The man waited. He searched the horizon, perturbed. What might there be farther on? Might there be beneath their feet another sky like the one they saw at night? What did animal blood taste like? With the pole he prodded the dog so they could move on. It wasn't long before Cain dashed off after another rabbit. Adam ran behind the dog, testing the swiftness of his legs. He tore the rabbit from Cain's jaws. The rabbit's head swung loosely from its body.

This time it was the man's turn to hide. He sat down beneath a tree. He closed his eyes. He sank his teeth into the fur. He tasted the blood, the meat beneath the skin. With his teeth and nails he tore off the skin and pulled off a leg. He ate the warm, bloody meat with the smell of musk.

He heard soft laughter. A mocking laugh.

"Look what you've become. Now you have to kill in order to eat."

Adam thought it was the voice inside him, but then he recognized the hoarse tones that were reminiscent of rolling stones. He saw the Serpent.

"It's you. I recognize you. What do you eat?"

"I have eaten mice, deer. Rabbit isn't bad. But look at you, who thought you were so special. Here you are, eating like any animal."

"Is that how we will survive in this world, eating each other?"

"Life feeding on death. Elokim flies into a rage and does these things: he condemns one kind of nature to live like another. But as you see, he said I would eat dirt, and you grass and thorns, but he changed his mind. Now he would rather we feed on each other."

"You know him very well."

"We have been together for a long time. As long as he exists, I will exist, too."

"You exist to contradict him."

"Without me he would find eternity intolerable. I provide him with surprises, the unpredictable. I have given you a gift," the Serpent added, hissing. "You will find it when you get back to the cave. It will help you eat, and keep warm. But you must hurry. I tried to warn Eve but she refused to listen. If you don't hurry, she will die."

A chill of alarm ran down Adam's spine. He felt his muscles tense, his hands clench. He yelled for Cain, and as fast as he legs would carry him started back toward the cave, carrying the remains of the rabbit to share with Eve.

As he ran across the meadow, he saw a pride of lions that roared ferociously in his direction. They had formed a circle around their prey to protect it. As slowly as he could, trying to convey that he had no intention of competing with them, Adam eased behind some rocks and then picked up his pace again. He was remembering how many large, strong beasts he had named. All of them hungry, he thought. Who would devour whom?

He still had some distance to cover when he saw the smoke and flames enveloping the cave and the fig trees. Someone had covered the stones that formed the entrance with brush and grasses. Fire was crackling, rising in tall flames. He stopped, not knowing what to do. Even before he had known fear, fire had intimidated him. Of all the elements, it was the most powerful and magnificent. To see it so close, to feel its heat and smoke, and to imagine Eve in it, filled him with terror and impotence. The dog raced around as if mad, barking and howling. Adam went as close as he could, braving the heat, covering his face with his hands. He, too, began to howl, to moan, to stomp the ground with his feet, calling and shouting to Eve. Smoke was choking him. It couldn't be that Elokim would allow the Serpent to kill her. He had said that the time of dying had not come. Adam yelled at the top of his lungs, cursing, pleading, possessed by the most absolute desperation.

"Elokim. Elokim!" he cried, circling around, looking toward the Garden.

In a very short time, he saw the Phoenix. It was flying swiftly, extending its enormous red and gold wings. Adam clenched his fists. What could the bird do to calm the fire? Dazed, he watched it light above the burning cave, its wings outspread. Immediately, the fire that had been spreading in many directions began to retreat and converge upon the body of the bird, as if it were a domesticated creature responding to an imperative call. The outline of the bird, the entire body, sucked in the fire, growing larger so it would all fit inside. The flames embraced it, licked its tongues over the feathers of the Phoenix without altering the bird's immobility. Finally, above the cave, the colossal bird, blazing like a sun, again opened its wings and lifted its head. Stupefied, unable to move, Adam contemplated the incandescent figure burning without being consumed, until, slowly, without changing its similarity to a magnificent statue, the Phoenix was reduced to a heap of ashes. The fire was out. The man emerged from his state of impotent terror and made his way, hopping back and forth over the charred branches of the fig trees, to the mouth of the cave. Steaming vapor issued from its walls, but the opening was clear. He found Eve, trembling, huddled beneath the spring where only a thread of water was still trickling down.

"It was the Serpent, Adam. She said that now that you had killed, it was appropriate for you to know fire. What did you do?"

"Let's go outside. I will explain everything, but not in here."

It was late afternoon. The sky was striped with shreds of

pink and purple. Eve's hot skin brushed against his. Adam was pained by what had happened to the Phoenix. They had believed it to be immortal, he thought. The fiery silhouette burned in his memory. Deeply moved, he showed the woman the ashen remains. While he was looking for leaves to clean the soot from her face and body, Eve sat down on some rocks. Her eyes were taking in the cave, the dead fig trees, when she noticed the hand of the wind softly stirring the bird's ashes. It lifted them and let them fall, again and again, as if it were seeking a way to put them in order before it carried them away. The pile of ashes on the rock swirled without dispersing; it changed color, slowly converted into red and gold feathers that as they spun about settled into a form that seemed to lie in the memory of the air. In an instant, the bird's head emerged from the feathers. Rising from ruin, as if recently awakened, the bird shook itself, and as it did its feathers were returned to their original arrangement. Jubilant, comprehending perhaps in that instant the cycle that its nature would repeat throughout eternity, the Phoenix spread its extraordinary wings and with a graceful push and joyful call, mounted into the air. Perplexed, Adam and Eve watched it fuse with the colors of dusk and be lost against the horizon.

"Don't you think that the same will happen to us if we die?"

"I don't know, Eve, I don't know."

The sun hid. The man and woman took refuge from the night among the rocks, in the open. They had tried to go back inside the cave, but the walls were emitting intense heat and burned their skin when they touched them. From where they were they could see an orange glow spilling from inside. Coals.

Adam put his arms around Eve. Her skin smelled of smoke. That duplicitous Serpent, he thought. Both friend and enemy. It confused him.

"We don't have anything to eat," said Eve, looking at the charred figs.

"I have something," said Adam. He got up and went to look for the rabbit he had left in the fork of a nearby tree. He set it before Eve. He awaited her reaction. Where he saw food, she saw a bloody, inert animal. She screamed and covered her eyes.

"It's dead, Adam. Or will it come back to life the way the Phoenix did?"

"No. It's dead."

She opened her eyes. She touched the flaccid skin, the animal's limp lifelessness; she stared at the opaque pupils.

"This is what you want me to eat? Death?"

"This morning the cat saw a bird. It killed it and ate it. Then Cain caught a rabbit, and he ate that. When I saw him catch another, I took it from him and brought it so we would have it to eat. We will have to kill other animals and eat them if we want to survive. The Serpent told me that. She has eaten mice and deer. We have to eat more than figs. The meat of the rabbit isn't bad. I tasted it."

"And you believe the Serpent, Adam? You think we have to kill in order to live?" Eve looked at him, incredulous, astounded.

"I know only that as soon as I saw the cat eat the bird, I knew that this is what we have to do. There are many rabbits, Eve."

Eve tilted her head back, clasping her hands behind her neck in a gesture of desperation.

"Who is the Other? Who is the Serpent? Who are these beings, Adam? What do they want of us? One deceives us; the other punishes us. They pretend to be our friends but they contradict each other. If eating a fruit has brought us this punishment, what do you think will happen if we kill to eat? I don't want to kill, Adam. How will we know what to kill and what not to? Kill to eat," she repeated with an expression of repugnance and amazement. "Whoever thought of such a thing?"

"I told you there are many rabbits. They must have been made for this purpose."

"I assure you that the rabbit you kill does not care in the least whether there are many more. And if another animal decides that we're *its* rabbits?"

"Day by day we will have to live and learn. I can't answer all your questions."

"You should not kill. My whole body tells me that. If death is such a punishment, why do we have to inflict it on others? It seems it is difficult for Elokim to put himself in our place, though he thinks that he knows what is best for us, but I can put myself in the place of the rabbit. Poor creature. Look at it, turned into waste."

"It isn't a matter of killing for killing's sake, but killing to survive."

"It wasn't that way in the Garden."

"You wanted to know Good and Evil. Perhaps this is evil. We will have to try it. If not, we will die."

"We are going to die whatever we do."

"Elokim said that our time hadn't come."

"So it seems to you that this is the evil we must try."

"Yes."

"But we are free, Adam, we can choose. If you think that we made one mistake, why should we make another? We have been left on our own. It's our decision how we want to live."

Adam stared at Eve for a long moment. He admired her vehemence. But she was the one who had brought them to this crossroad. She'd had no fear of knowing Good and Evil and now she was afraid of what they would have to do to live.

"You ate the fruit."

"I wanted to know, Adam. Now I know more than I did when we were in the Garden. That's why I'm asking you not to kill."

"If we hadn't eaten the fruit, it's possible that we would never have had to kill, but now we're alone. I can't do what you ask. I, too, know what I have to do. Maybe it isn't up to you to kill. Maybe that is why we're different."

"It may be, Adam. Think that if you want."

"I am larger and stronger than you. I feel responsible for our surviving."

"I feel responsible for looking after you. And it seems that I will have to begin by protecting you from yourself. We are *not* animals, Adam."

"How do you know that? The only thing that differentiates us from them is that we speak."

"And have knowledge."

"I know that we have to eat. The animals know that, too. You are the only one it bothers."

"It troubles me to have to kill."

"That is how it is. We didn't make it that way."

"You will have to harden yourself to do it. You will learn to be cruel."

"That may be evil, Eve, but evil is also part of knowledge."

Eve thought with nostalgia of the light and quiet of the Garden. Of eternity. She recalled the repose of her spirit, the simple thoughts of a mind untouched by alarm, by weeping, by anguish or rage; that feeling of floating along on the surface of the water like a leaf.

"If we hadn't eaten the fruit," she said, looking Adam in the eye, "I would never have tasted a fig, or an oyster. I wouldn't have seen the Phoenix rise from its ashes. I wouldn't have known night. I wouldn't have learned that I feel alone when you leave me, and I wouldn't have felt how my body—so cold, even in the heart of the fire—filled with warmth when I heard you calling me. I would have gone on seeing you naked without being disturbed. I would never have known how much I like it when like a fish you slip inside me to invent the ocean."

"And I wouldn't have known that I don't like for you to be hungry. To me it seems cruel to watch you grow pale and not do anything to prevent it. I didn't decide that things should be this way, Eve. I learn from what I find around me."

Adam had nothing to add. Eve, too, was silent. Why did they think so differently? she wondered. Which of the two would prevail? Out in the open, near the rocks around the cave, she curled up beside him and later, straddling Adam with the waning moon above her head, caused the man to forget hunger and the need to kill.

In the early morning they returned to the cave. The intense heat had given way to a pleasantly warm emanation. On the sand of the grotto a few stones were still faintly glowing. Thoughtlessly, Adam dropped the rabbit. In a bit, the smell of the roasting meat started his saliva flowing. On the fire, the meat turned golden and was easier to sink his teeth into. He would have to learn to control the fire's intensity, he thought. Like everything else, it contained both good and evil.

The woman observed him, but kept her distance.

THE NEXT DAY IT was Eve who went out to explore. She chose to go alone. "You mustn't go very far," he said; "you don't want to find yourself somewhere you can't get back from." What made him think that she couldn't come and go as easily as he? She smiled. And went out.

She noticed that the sun was softly filtering through a cloud-covered sky. She walked toward the river, planning to find some way to cross to the greenness on the other shore. The dog followed her through the meadow of tall yellow grasses. It ran ahead of her sniffing the ground, stirring up rabbits that fled in every direction. There were many, it was true. She imagined their tiny hearts beating with fright. A falcon flew very low, snatched up one, and flew away with it. It will kill it. It will eat it, she thought. She remembered the scent of animal flesh. The vision of live creatures eating one another was repugnant. The blood. The dog's teeth. The torment of the sacrificed animals. All so sad. What good could result if life fed on death? Who had arranged it that way? What would she and Adam do if another animal tried to kill them? She refused to accept that this was the only way to sustain themselves. The earth produced figs and fruits. If it fed birds and elephants, it had to offer sweet and benign nourishment. Ah, how she missed the white petals of the Garden!

She came to the river. She stopped to look at it. She imagined a gigantic eye very far from there weeping crystalline water. The river moved so swiftly and yet it had no purpose other than to flow, just flow. She listened to its murmuring. Maybe birds died in the river and continued to sing within it. The inexpressive, mute stones were soft and meek beneath the water. The river came from far away. It disappeared on the horizon. High atop the mountain from which they had thrown themselves into the void, she remembered having seen two long strands of water twisting across the landscape until they grew small in the distance. Someday they would have to follow this water and see where it went.

She walked beneath the shade of the trees, breathing in with pleasure the scent of growing things. Squirrels, birds, insects abounded. The dog was sniffing everything. It stopped to urinate. From the riverbank, Eve crossed to a little island, balancing on stones that rose above the surface. The dog swam. Eve, too, sank into the water to swim to the far shore. There she collected fruit in a palm leaf, anything that seemed fleshy and edible. The countryside was greener and more lush on that shore; there were luxuriant trees and some small palms displaying clusters of fruits she pulled off, enchanted with her find. She also found some tall golden grasses crowned with small hard grains she also tasted. She wandered along, possessed of a strange energy, like a deer, looking here and there, no longer contemplative but moved by a clear purpose of finding in the nature around her things that could be transformed and useful to them. She tore off long, pale leaves. She tied them together to hold what she had gathered. She picked husks, seeds, flowers, examining them all, sure she was surrounded with clues that with patience and care she would be able to decipher. The previous night, looking at the feathers of the Phoenix, she had in her imagination constructed feathered robes for her and for Adam, but she had found only a few feathers scattered about the ground.

On the way back with her small load, she had a moment's dismay. She would lose everything when she crossed back to the small island. She saw branches floating in the current, and figured out that by using vines she was carrying to tie together two large, dry pieces of wood, she could put together a small frame to transport her booty. The dog lay down in the shade to wait while she worked. Finally, Eve reached the other side, shivering but happy. And she knew that what she had done that day was good.

CHAPTER 13

*A*DAM HAD KILLED MORE RABBITS. HE HAD SKINNED them. Eve was saddened when she returned and saw the array of skins—stiff, emptied silhouettes—laid out on the rocks in the sun. She found Adam sprawled inside the cave, his face concentrated on clinging to sleep, the remains of his feast on the ground beside the fire, where pieces of dry wood were burning. The cat lying impassively beside him raised its head to look at her. The dog took possession of a few bones and went to lie down in a corner of the cave.

Eve opened her bundle of fruit and ate dates and oranges.

"The land on the other side of the river is like the Garden," she told Adam when he woke up. "There are a lot of trees and fruits. Look what I found. You won't have to kill more rabbits."

"Did you see how many I brought? I used a burning stick to light a fire on one side of the meadow, and took up a post on the other. They came running. If you had been with me, we would have had even more."

He smiled with satisfaction and pride.

"Why did you want so many?"

"We will use the skins to cover ourselves, and we will not want for food."

"I told you that there is fruit in abundance on the other side of the river."

"We can't go too far from here, Eve. We have to wait close to the Garden in case the Other regrets it and changes his mind. Come see."

He got up and led her outside to a place in the rocks where he had laid two rabbits, not skinned, on a clean flat rock.

"I've put out this offering to the Other. I want him to know that we are grateful that he intervened and sent the Phoenix to save you from the fire. He has continued to look out for us. Maybe he will forgive us."

"It's one thing to prevent our dying and another to be in a mood to let us return."

"Look, you were mistaken when you thought that eating the fruit would not amount to much. It may be that you are mistaken again."

"And if he doesn't come to take the rabbits?"

"We will take them to him. We will bring him an offering every day to soften his heart."

That night, Eve felt that sleep would be slow to come. She opened her eyes in the dark and saw the eyes of the cat shining, unblinking, along with the reddish glow of the low fire Adam had fed with dry grasses and twigs so it wouldn't go out. She did not understand cruelty, but the word tasted bitter on her tongue. She closed her eyes. She searched deep into her anguish for the difference between the blood that flowed from her most intimate self and the blood of the rabbits. In her mind's eye, the sea reappeared, and also the long, quiet beach on which the waves sang their endless song. On the distant rocks she saw a figure. She thought it was Adam, and walked toward it. The face of another like herself surprised her. That this other recognized her and knew her name amazed her even more. Unlike herself, who was barely covered with the crude, ragged skin that served as clothing, this woman was enveloped in a feather garment that fell softly over her body. Eve could hear that she was talking, but the wind carried away her words. Eve wanted to hear her, and walked closer, struggling against the strong wind, which had become dense, and white. Her mouth filled with salt, but she did not give up. She wanted to know who had so suddenly appeared in her solitude. At last she was able to break free from the wind that had entrapped her, and she fell forward on the woman. With the embrace, the face she was looking at dissolved. When Eve regained her balance she was alone on the beach, sitting in place of the other, wearing the feather robe, gazing at the sea.

"Adam, where do we go when we sleep? Who are the ones like us who live inside our dreams? Last night I saw another like me on the beach. She may be there. We should go look for her."

Adam said that he had dreamed of others like him. This didn't mean that they existed. Dreams were what they themselves wanted to see.

Adam went outside to see whether Elokim had taken away the rabbits. There was nothing now on the stone, but up on the crag that crowned the solitary mountain he saw two large buzzards, biding their time. He ran to pick up the skins he had put out to cure, instinct telling him that it was not Elokim who had taken away his offering.

"We will take it to the Garden," he said when he returned to the cave.

Eve gave him oranges and berries to taste. He ate slowly, savoring the sweet juice and flesh of the fruit. She collected the seeds to plant later, so that, like the figs, they would be converted into trees. They gathered dry branches to revive the fire. Adam threw a string of sacrificed rabbits over his shoulder and they set out toward the Garden.

It was hot. In the distance the sky was gray, filled with smoke, as if the other half of the earth, the part they couldn't see, was burning. They recalled visions from their first days: disturbances and splendors they had contemplated without worry. The signs of cataclysms and rumbling that made the ground shake beneath their feet now terrified them. Eve pressed close to Adam. What was out there? Farther on? she wondered. She questioned whether someday they might know what the distance held. Adam held her close. She was smaller, her body more delicate. He wondered why. He wondered if she could be right to think that she was with him to protect him from himself. He often was afraid to leave her alone. He feared the way she dreamed, how she left his side without moving. Her eyes surprised him, seeing signals that for him went by unperceived, and her skin, which like the nose of the dog and the cat, sensed what was to happen. Many nights, watching her sleep, he wanted to wake her and hurt her. He could not help the rancor he held for the peculiar way with which, unlike him, she was connected with the Earth, like a tree without roots. It amazed him that she barely lamented having eaten the fruit of the Tree. She insisted that it wasn't she but the Other who was responsible, and she refused to accept her part of the blame, the dangerous force of her curiosity. She could still put them at risk if she continued to insist on going farther from the Garden, arguing that they would never return. He could not resign himself to accept that. More than of cataclysms and the unknown, he was afraid of himself, of what he was prepared to do in order to survive in this hostile land. He was afraid of hunger, and of the ferocity with which he had killed the rabbits one by one, crushing their heads with a rock. A person had to be cruel to kill. She was not mistaken.

They knew the way to the Garden by heart, and for that reason they could search their innermost thoughts as they walked through the meadow where the wheat grew tall and golden—without their having yet envisioned the bread its grains contained.

Distant smoke carried by the wind clouded the light of day, dimming the outlines of the land. As always happened when they approached the Garden, sadness entered through their feet and rose up their bodies like a climbing vine. In their memories, nostalgia intensified the color, weight, and aromas of their recollections.

THIS TIME ADAM WAS the first to notice the changes. Eve was walking with lowered head, concentrating on repressing her revulsion at the odor of the dead rabbits. The sound of his voice startled her and she looked up.

"Its fading, Eve, it's fading!" he exclaimed with anguish.

Eve looked. She stumbled slightly when the surprise at what

she saw combined with the sensations of her the body. Adam ran to support her. Leaning on him, she saw a broad band of light within which, as if suctioned by enormous force, the precipice was closing. The Earth was being joined again, but everything that had been the Garden was ascending, dissolving in a resplendent mist, as if a hidden ferment was boiling up from the depths of the ground and vaporizing the trees, the orchids, the climbing passion flowers. Vegetation was being converted into drawn-out silhouettes that lengthened toward the sky in vertical strokes of green filled with pale vibrating shades of red, blue, violet, and yellow, as if suddenly the Garden was yielding to its unrecognized vocation: rainbow. The shapes of tree trunks, shrubs, everything closer to the ground, was the same, but the majestic branches of the Tree of Life and the darker Tree of Knowledge of Good and Evil, as well as the foliage and colors in the uppermost part of the trees, were separating from the surface, creating the effect of rain that was rising instead of falling, vibrant, trembling, holding within it every tone of green; it was like seeing the image of a pool that someone was gently and slowly drawing up into the sky.

Eve opened and closed her eyes to be sure that the vision was not the result of her fainting spell. She did not know the word *farewell*, but she felt it. She thought that the death they had been promised would be something like this. The landscape and the colors would fade, the original site of memories would vanish, and they would be left defenseless, numb, alone, impotently watching what was, or could have been, disappear.

She was enraged by such a cruel design.

However, it was perhaps time for the Garden to be gone,

time to accept once and for all the reality for which they had been created and in which they would have to live. In the midst of her indignation she felt the clarity of Elokim's thought expanding inside her. She and Adam were not the beginning, but the perfect end he had wanted to see before emboldening himself to grant them freedom, she felt he said. Someday their descendents would undertake a return to the Garden of Eden. Eve envisioned a knot at her core untying, separating from her link by link: rough beings making their way, overcoming obstacle after obstacle in search of the Garden, that vision of splendor she planted in their memory. She understood the urgency and hope caused by her glimpse of the confused, multitudinous images she was still incapable of deciphering. She had seen the groping search of her descendants, the circular road that they would have to travel until they sighted the outlines of the trees beneath which she had drawn her first breath. She wished she and Adam could have kept the small, perfect parcel of ground that would forever point toward her with its accusing finger. She realized that it would serve very little to allude to her innocence. Her guilt was also part of the designs of Elokim and the Serpent.

She came back to herself. Adam was shaking her.

"You were right," he moaned. "He is destroying it. We will never be able to return, or eat of the Tree of Life."

The man put his arms around Eve's waist, sobbing, disconsolate. He had harbored the certainty that they would return to the Garden. Now that he had killed, death inspired terror. Every night his anxiety grew. He touched himself when he woke; he filled his lungs to be sure of the air, the scent of the earth, Eve's presence at his side. He gave thanks for light, the water of his eyes, the firmness of his skin, his muscles and bones, even the animal functions that had initially repelled him. And now Elokim was forcing him to contemplate the end of his beginnings. Just like the foliage of the trees, so his life and Eve's would dissolve, as would the ocean, river, fire, or Phoenix their eyes had seen.

They did not have to consult each other to know that they would wait there until the Garden disappeared completely. Awed by the spectacle, they found a place among some rocks, fluctuating between amazement and consternation. Ribbons of color fluttered in the wind, breaking into vertical lines of changing hues; from the tops of the trees, flocks of birds rose into the sky, scattering in all directions; the male and female Phoenix left, flying toward the sun. Their magnificent iridescent red and gold wings caught fire in the distance and filled the air with flames. Eve had the clear sensation that time had stopped. She did not know if it was because everything was happening at a dizzying pace, while they and everything around them held their breath. Even the insects the dead rabbit had attracted seeming to be floating in the air, immobile. Adam's movements, as he fanned them away with a handful of wheat, seemed to her exasperatingly slow.

"Eve, do you think we could go in one last time? The precipice has closed over."

"There's nothing left of the Tree of Life but the roots. Elokim will know that we can no longer eat from it and live forever," she replied.

"I don't want to die."

"What did the rabbits do when you killed them?"

"They struggled, but afterward they were quiet."

"Maybe that is all there is: struggle and then quiet."

"And afterward, will there be another Garden?"

"And what would we do there with the knowledge of Good and Evil we have acquired?"

"I don't know, Eve. I don't know. Do we try now to go in once more? I would like to go in."

They approached with caution. They were afraid they would be harassed by the whip of fire. Only a few solid traces of the Garden remained. Nothing hindered them. They walked among silhouettes of trees and plants. In the reverberation of the air there were still traces of certain aromas, even the song of birds. Color, like foam, clung briefly to their skin. The Garden was saying good-bye, licking them like a dog.

In the spot where Adam remembered waking with Eve at his side, they found three small plants whose roots were still locked in the soil. Carefully, they took them up to carry back and plant, thinking that beneath their shade they could again have the illusion of being in the Garden of Eden.

They went to the center of the Garden, to the site of the Tree of Life and Tree of Knowledge. The bands of color were now above their heads, forming a dense string of intense bright green lights. Beautiful, said Eve. Beauty. That is how it is called. She was happy at having found the right word. She had looked for it more than once in the world of her exile that little by little was capturing her with its violent dusks, its plains, its rivers. Beauty appeared if the eye knew to recognize it. Perhaps it existed even in death. Perhaps death was not so bad. She shook her head, looked at her hands. Her hair and her finger-nails had grown. How long would their lives last outside the eternal time of the Garden?

CHAPTER 14

THE WALK BACK TO THE CAVE WAS SLOW, SPIRIT-less. It was true that for a long time the Garden had been inaccessible to them. But they had known where it was. They could see it, even if from afar. That knowing was a strange consolation. It marked a point of departure, their origin. As the Garden disappeared, they were left to the mercy of remembered images, memories that over time they would confuse with dreams. Adam walked ahead. Eve hung back, sunk in her meditations. Once more she recalled the Serpent's words: "He grows bored. He creates planets, constellations, and then forgets them."

She had just been thinking of that when she heard the hissing voice calling her. She looked toward where a faint cloud of dust was rising. The Serpent was hurriedly dragging herself along to catch up.

"He didn't take you with him? Did he abandon you, too?" Eve asked.

"He wants to be alone. I think he's sad. But he is the one

responsible for that. He creates his own mirages. Look how he made you in his own image and likeness but did not dare give you more freedom than that of knowing your limits. Although I must say that—except for me—there are very few I have seen him share so much power with. The Earth belongs to you and Adam now. You can re-create it, define Good and Evil as you please."

"As we please?"

"He won't be around. He will not live day by day the way you live; he will not be able to whisper into your ears all the time."

Eve was pensive.

"We will have to learn to recognize Good and Evil. We ate of the fruit of the Tree."

"Aha."

"Eating animals, killing them, is that good or evil?"

"That Adam is hungry, is that good or evil?" the Serpent asked with irony.

"He could eat other things."

"He believes that it isn't good to eat nothing but fruits and nuts. It doesn't satisfy his hunger."

"Other animals kill, too. The cat and the dog."

"And they know nothing. Good and Evil are extremes. There are many stages between them."

"You're confusing me."

"It's a confusing matter. It's the search that you wanted to undertake."

"To me, killing to eat is not good."

"Don't do it. Convince Adam."

"I've tried, but he insists."

"Insist more."

"It would be pointless. Hunger is anguishing, and punctual, like the sun and the moon."

"Stop, then. Don't judge him."

"But it will have consequences."

"You decided to eat from the Tree. That, too, had consequences. Now go. You've lagged behind. Adam is looking for you. He worries when he doesn't see you."

Back in the cave, Eve curled up into a heavy sleep that stayed with her for many days. In her world without a past, and almost without memories, her dreams were repeated without ever being the same. Elokim, the Serpent, the Phoenix, the rabbits, oranges, berries, the sea, death; eating and being naked, one inside the other. Adam did not want her sad drowsiness to stick to his skin. He left her dreaming and busied himself. He went to the bank of the river to look for the fine plants with thin, flexible stems. With the thorns from a shrub, he made holes in the dry rabbit skins and passed the plant fiber in and out until he made a covering that would protect him from the intense pain that resulted when his genitals were banged around. To soften the skins, he soaked them in mud for several days. He had noticed that the dirtier the mud, the softer they became. Using the softest skins, he stitched something for Eve that would cover her shoulders, breasts, and genitals. He hunted more rabbits, and he hunted timid pheasants. He jumped into the river to catch fish, but they slipped from his hands. He gathered eggs from the nests of birds. He followed the river downstream, crossed to the island, and explored the place where Eve had found the oranges and berries. The woman was eating almost nothing. She talked aloud in her dreams and her stomach returned almost everything he urged her to eat.

The fire and the odor of meat attracted other animals. The dog barked at night, and Adam heard threatening roars and growls. Eve did not want to see it, but now there were many animals that satisfied their hunger by eating one another. Adam searched for stones, chipped them, and with them dug the ground and at the entrance to the cave placed several rows of shafts to keep out unwelcome visitors. It astonished him to find within himself answers to the puzzles necessity confronted him with. He bound sharpened stones to long wood poles to increase his power. He tried to catch a pair of deer. He and Cain chased them, but they quickly outran the man and the dog.

The full moon again appeared in the night sky, but Eve did not bleed.

"My body is changing, Adam. Look at my breasts, how large and heavy they've become. And I am sleepy all the time, and everything I eat turns to poison inside me."

Adam refused to talk about those things with her. He pretended not to see any of the things she pointed out to him. What he was seeing frightened him, and he found no way to explain it.

"You feel worn down because you sleep so much. Come with me tomorrow morning. It will do you good to get into the river. We will try to catch a fish, or we will go back to the sea to look for oysters."

He showed her the garment he had stitched. She got up. She was dirty. She smelled. Her hair was tangled. She thought of the watery meat of the oysters and felt hungry. He had kept the fire burning. He was changing, too, she thought. He had stopped complaining; he had stopped having any hope. Without the alternative of the Garden, he had turned to the skill of his hands and to his own intuition.

"You have been very busy." She smiled.

"I went to the other side of the river. We can go there together if you want."

"I want to get into the water of the river, but I would like to go to the sea."

He fed the fire. He put the stones he had been sharpening into a kind of pouch he'd made from another of the skins. Certain stones were very good for cutting, he told her. They started out walking. Adam did not know how to tell her how long she'd been sleeping. When the fig tree burned he had stopped making the notches he used to count the days, but he told her he had spent many nights waiting for her to come back from where she was wandering. In that time the air had grown cold and the leaves of the trees were falling to the ground, yellow and dry. Perhaps soon everything they'd seen would diffuse and dissolve like the Garden. The land certainly looked desolate. The greens were growing pale, and the light of the sun fell on them soft and mild.

"What are the animals doing? Have you seen them?"

"From a distance. They come near, but only during the night. Then I hear their formidable breathing outside the cave. I hear them but I don't understand them."

"And does that make you afraid?"

"I'm afraid they're thinking of eating me, the same I'm thinking of them. If I could lay a hand on a larger animal, I wouldn't have to go hunt rabbits or pheasants every day. It's more difficult every time because I think they are on to the tricks I use to catch them."

"I don't know how you do it. Does it please you to think you are stronger and cleverer?"

"Yes, I know what I have to do, and that amazes me. I confront a difficulty and after thinking about it for a while, I suddenly know how to solve it. I see possibilities, I test them, and one of them always works."

"Then something more than killing moves you."

"Killing! That isn't what it's about. It's about surviving. I am smaller than many animals, but I have an advantage because I can predict their movements. They, on the other hand, have no imagination. More than words, I think that is what makes us different from them. That and sadness, Eve. It pains me when I remember the animals walking with me in the Garden and I realize that now all I think about is eating them. It's wrong of you to believe that it isn't difficult for me."

"It's cold outside the cave, Adam. Do you think the sun is going out?"

"I think that when the Garden disappeared the world turned sad. I hope the sun doesn't fade, Eve. We will have to make more offerings to Elokim so that he will take pity on us."

They came to the river. The vegetation on the banks was still intensely green. The water was darker and very cold. Eve sat on the grass and began to chew it. Chew, eat—soon she, too, would succumb to necessity, and to hunger. She would no longer judge Adam, as the Serpent had counseled. Which was worse, hunger or death? Her bones were floating in her body, and now they were visible beneath her skin. She could see the arc of her ribs, her protruding hip bones, her knees.

Only her belly had swelled. There was nothing left to do but resign herself to existing the way all the animals did that ate one another. Even so, there were many that simply grazed. She, however, could not eat grass all day they way they did. Her stomach wouldn't tolerate it. Green vomit was bitter, and inevitable after she ate the stems and flowers Adam brought to her because it was what he saw the deer and gazelles and sheep eat. She got up and went over to the water. Slowly, she slipped down into the current. With her arms crossed over her chest, holding her breath, she sank down into the icy water. The sensation was sharply painful but at the same time pleasurable. Her body folded into itself, but it also awakened; her blood flowed more swiftly. She gave a push with her feet and hands; she swam a little. Her long hair floated around her. A silvery fish approached and began to feed among the dark strands. It swam in and out as if these were the branches of a submarine plant. Other fish followed. Eve was suddenly surrounded by a mulititude of brilliant fish that darted around her without fear, brushing against her. Without thinking, she lifted a hand and ran her fingers along the back of one of the largest fish. The creature permitted it, and after swimming in a circle returned for more caresses. She tried taking one in her hand, and the fish lay quiet in her fingers. It was offering itself to her. It wanted her to catch it. She looked up and saw Adam on the bank, gesticulating, urging her to take the fish and throw them in his direction.

She clasped the largest one firmly, holding it in the middle. With a swift move, she threw it in Adam's direction, avoiding thinking, feeling the creature's vital palpitations. Fish kept brushing against her, as if they wanted her to do the same with them. She took another. She threw it to Adam. She did that four, five times. She was shivering, numb with cold, moved by the mute, gentle ritual of the fish delivering themselves to her as if they knew she needed them.

Adam had learned the secret of fire. He put dry twigs together and then struck two stones for a long time until a tiny spark leaped out and lit the wood. Eve looked at the five dead fish. She saw their open eyes. She held one in her hand and spoke to it, asking forgiveness. Then, mechanically, her eyes lost, she began to tear off scales with her fingernails, which had grown long and sharp, then handed the fish to Adam.

She ate the white meat with her eyes closed. It was soft, sweet, like the petals of Paradise.

CHAPTER 15

S LOWLY, EVE RECOVERED HER STRENGTH. FROM THE mushrooms with intricate skirts that grew in the dense vegetation along the banks of the river, she drew the idea of knotting the fibrous plants to make a net for catching fish. When she ate them, she tried not to picture their agile fins moving in the current. In order not to feel guilty, she convinced herself that water creatures didn't suffer the same death as land animals. She imagined that they traveled from one state to another with the same calm in which they passed their lives floating and swimming in silence. She dreamed that the fish she ate swam in her stomach, in the round refuge growing day by day in her belly.

She wanted to go back to the sea. The memory of the oysters, the thought of finding the woman glimpsed in her dreams, the quiet lowing of the waves, the wish to walk alone and avoid the man's insistence on going everywhere with her, possessed her mind. She waited till Adam went off one morning, and then she started walking.

She liked the sensation of having nothing with her but her thoughts. She descended from the cave and looked at the mountain rising above it, rocky and steep to the peak, with bushes whose thorns she still remembered raking her skin. As she climbed down, she could see on the plain a flock of small long-necked animals with small horns. Goats, she thought. The creatures from the garden had scattered. Adam had told her that he'd seen elephants, giraffes, and zebras disappear beyond the horizon, moving as if, at last, someone had told them where to go. Some animals disappeared, and others returned from the stampede of the first days. Some did not mind being seen; others prowled in a crouch, like Adam, hunting creatures smaller or less ferocious. She thought of the hyenas but put them out of her mind in order not to become frightened.

Across the plain, the mountains stood out in the calm, warm day. The green along the riverbanks was beautiful. To reach the sea, she would have to cross a wooded valley to the other side of the mountain, climb some hills, and then walk across a flat, desolate expanse where groups of palm trees grew. With luck, she would be back at the cave by dusk.

She walked toward the open space on a slope of the mountain, until she entered the woods. The land descended abruptly. She tried not to lose sight of the hill she would have to climb in order to see the sea on the other side, but soon she found herself among tree trunks and dense foliage. Unlike the forever-glowing light of the Garden, intervals of sunlight in the depths of the forest sometimes faded to dark shadow. The air smelled faintly of dampness, and her footsteps crunched on the leaves and stirred insects and small creatures that scurried away as she passed. Taking her time, enjoying herself, she stopped to look at centipedes, a lizard, a turtle with an orange shell.

She wondered how much of eternity Elokim had needed to create all that, whether he had paid attention to the details or if the creatures he imagined, once conceived, had taken charge of inventing for themselves the best way to live in such different places. She was shocked that she hadn't asked about such things in the Garden. She was aware of the placidity with which she had accepted everything that existed: she, too, part of a beauty that never questioned itself.

She thought she had walked long enough to reach the hill, but she continued to go from dark to light, from light to dark. She attempted to locate the spot from which she had descended, calculating that she must be at least halfway across the valley. She looked around her. She thought she recognized certain trees by the climbing vines that grew on their trunks but realized that the perception was illusory, and that the trees reflected one another like one of those repeated dreams incessantly circling around the same thing. She started retracing her steps, thinking she would follow her tracks out, but after a short distance they vanished. She was not dispirited. She told herself that all she had to do was decide to walk in one direction and not deviate and she would get out of there. The valley was not very broad, and at some moment she would have to emerge. She walked on without stopping. Several times she thought she was approaching the end of the forest, but no. She was lost, she thought, furious with herself. Her fury turned into fear and despair when, after repeated attempts to retrace her steps or to try a different route, she noticed that the daylight was fading. She was hungry and thirsty. She saw a large, tall tree covered with small fruit. She pulled off a few. She studied them in the palm of her hand, and she recognized them. They were figs. Smaller and yellower than the ones from the fig tree by the cave, or the one in the Garden, but nevertheless figs. She sat down at the foot of the tree. She would rest, she thought. She would rest and eat.

What would Adam do when he couldn't find her? What would she do if she couldn't find her way out of this place? The sounds increased as the light faded. Cicadas and crickets emitted their long, sustained twilight songs. She heard the hoarse croaking of frogs and sensed the awakening of nocturnal butterflies. She might have to spend the night and wait for the following day. If up till now she hadn't succeeded in making her way out, she couldn't imagine how she would be able to do so in the darkness. Suddenly she heard a great jabbering and felt a commotion in the tree branches. A band of monkeys made their appearance. They were swinging through the branches, but gradually they settled to devote themselves to the fruit. Eve observed that they weren't the small monkeys with pale faces and slender, agile bodies she used to see in her explorations with Adam, the ones that had always made her think of spiders, perhaps because of the designs they made as they swung to and fro. These were large animals, with broad backs and arms. She saw their gleaming eyes, looking at her.

Strange, she thought. She didn't remember having seen animals like them in the Garden. After a long pause filled with shrieking, the monkeys reached an accord and one by one they came toward her. The most daring came down from the tree and surrounded her, silently. From time to time one of them emitted a sharp, repeated sound. Eve was impressed by their expressive, almost human faces, and the sweetness of the eyes that were looking her over with curiosity. She had never felt looked at in this way by any other animal. One of the male monkeys, the largest, the one with most authority, came nearer. She smiled at it, not knowing what to do. She was more fascinated than afraid, wondering what the animal had in mind. It stood up tall and held out one of its arms and softly, with its large, wrinkled hand, touched the hair that fell around her face. The other monkeys began to leap about and make little shrieks.

The monkey that had touched her took her hand. It wanted her to climb the tree with it. She said no, shook her head. Had it confused her with one of them? Surprised, Eve tried to communicate with it by signs, indicating that climbing was not her way of moving through the world. She could only walk, and could not find a way to get out of there. The monkey watched her intently. She turned around to show it that she did not have a tail, gesticulating so it would understand that she could not climb trees. After a while, several of the monkeys climbed back up the tree trunk and squatted in the branches. Finally, they all left. It was totally dark in the forest when she realized she was again alone. Later, cuddled against the tree, resigned to the night, she felt that they were throwing figs, and she saw the monkey that had touched her before. It came very close. It jumped about and scratched its head, making little shrieks as if it wanted to tell her something. She watched it start away from the tree, moving between the trees, resting its weight on its arms and legs. It looked at her and waved its arms. She took a while to understand, but she got up and began to follow it.

———————

It was far into the night when Eve saw the cave in the moonlight. She found Adam beside the fire. He was hoarse from yelling, from calling her so long. He had looked for her at the river, near the mark left by the Garden, and had only recently come back to the cave, hoping she had returned.

"I tried to go to the sea. I wanted to see it," she said. She told him how she had lost her way, her attempts to find her way back, and her encounter with the monkeys.

"One of them showed me the way. It led me to the edge of the forest. It left me there, as if it had understood me. Do you think it understood me, Adam?"

"I don't know, woman," said Adam, embracing her.

He slept with his ear on Eve's belly, clinging to her legs, thinking that the only Paradise he wanted was to be near her like this, listening to the sea that was growing inside her, where it seemed to him he could hear the song of dolphins.

CHAPTER 16

*E*VE WAS AFRAID THAT HER INTERNAL SEA WOULD drown her. The creatures in it were more and more rest-less; they beat against the walls of her belly and milled about under her ribs. The round moon she had inside her just kept growing. Moving around with the weight she was carry-ing was more uncomfortable every day. She wondered if at some moment she would come to a standstill, condemned to exist like some grotesque plant that had a memory of being a woman. She did not know what it was that was so agitated inside her, or if this state was temporary or permanent. Her greatest fear was that one day she would vomit up a marine monster, a new species, that would eat her and Adam and then inhabit alone the land where surviving perhaps required more ferocity than they were capable of.

"I have seen other animals swollen like you, Eve. You aren't the only one. The goats are like that. I saw a wolf, too. Some-thing will come out of you."

"Little rabbits," Eve laughed. "Only rabbits make more rabbits. Will we multiply, Adam? Is it our reflection that is forming inside me? Sometimes I think that I am filled with water, and that all the fish I've eaten will come out to prey on us."

"I was never small. Neither were you. Our reflection wouldn't fit inside you."

"There are little rabbits. They grow later. What I have inside is moving."

"It must be the white petals, or fish to feed whatever appears when we sleep."

"And you, Adam, don't you feel anything?"

"I'm worried, Eve. I wonder if one day we will do something other than think of not being hungry or how not to die of the cold. I can't think of anything else."

In the frozen world of winter, Adam found himself forced to forage among the prey left by other animals, competing with vultures for the spoils. Sometimes he was surprised to find whole chunks of meat among the bones. He imagined that the large quadrupeds—the tigers, bears, lions—still held in the silence of their memories the bond he had forged with them in the Garden, and that this was their way of showing him they had not forgotten everything. He was overjoyed with these finds, but he also wept. At the same time he was salivating, thinking about eating, he wailed. He remembered the time when it would have been impossible for him to imagine a world populated by creatures that were a threat to one another and driven to mutual distrust by the necessity of surviving. He wept as he gobbled down food, tearing off meat, moaning from the hunger of days, graceless, humiliated, and at the same time elated to be able to go back to the cave and feed Eve, the cat, and the dog.

Eve was touched when she saw him return. Hunger had at last brought her to try whatever he found. She asked no questions. She laid the pieces of meat on the fire and ate almost without taking a breath. Often while she chewed, she cursed Elokim. Her heavy body prevented her from going with Adam, and she had to resign herself to going out mornings to collect fallen branches to feed the fire, and during the day to stitching the skins they wore for warmth.

The solitude, however, suited her well. She didn't mind being alone as long as she was confident that he would return, and she preferred not to doubt that. Despite the hyenas, Adam was safe. "Don't be afraid," she told him, "the hyenas have moved on." "I'm not afraid," he told her, "you are the one who hasn't recovered from that fright." Eve knew that it was her own fear talking. The encounter with the hyenas had stored in her memory the horror of confirming the end of their complicity with the animals, the need to know anew everything they thought they knew. When Eve was alone in the cave, her sadness sometimes overwhelmed her. Again and again she went over every experience she had lived, and the reasoning that had led her to bite into the fig. The visions, the assurance with which she had believed in the History that supposedly she would inaugurate, filled her with anguish and rage against herself. The landscape sometimes reminded her of the beauty of the Garden, but beauty could not compensate for the pain of injured skin when it bled; it was not as strong as hunger and thirst and cold.

One day the need to shake off anguish caused her to invent a way to be able to look at it and to set it aside. From then on, she realized that even her sadness had a purpose.

Eve discovered that with the dry, blackened wood from the fire she could draw black lines on the walls of the cave. She began by testing the effect on one of the smoothest walls. As time passed, the first clumsy lines became more fluid. As she tried to transfer images from her memory onto the wall, her arm filled with warmth and her enthusiasm grew. Her hand lost its timidity and flew along, drawing figures with the charcoal. As she drew she experienced a different, inexplicable contentment that had the quality of making her feel less alone. Everything that was hidden within her came out to keep her company. Then she drew other figures: the deer sighted among the trees, the magnificent bison lowering its large head. With the red powder from the rocks she made the sun. She sketched the course of the river and the stones on its banks, and it was as if the murmur of the water were sounding in her ears.

She also depicted Adam in his explorations. She made him tall, monumental, larger and stronger than any animal he might come across. She drew him crossing through benevolent country, sleeping in the shelter of rocks where nothing menaced him, sure that reality would find a way to resemble her drawings.

"And I who spent nights afraid that hyenas or coyotes would devour me," he had said, mocking himself to veil the awe he felt when he saw the images of reality on the wall.

It wasn't long, however, before he was aware of the power of the figures. To envision the drawings, to know that Eve would be sketching out his return, comforted him. Every time he came back, he narrated the details of his adventures so that when she drew them, she would live them with him. He marveled as he watched her hand move, as from her fingers flowed lines that, without being a deer or a tiger, seemed to possess the essence of a deer or a tiger. In the firelight, Adam found pleasure in telling her about his forays. Often he yielded to the temptation to add his fantasies to reality. He enjoyed seeing her hanging on his words. It was like taking her with him, and living all of it at her side.

Toward the end of winter, thin and weak, the man stopped going out from the cave. Day after day all they ate was straw, plants, and insects. Two pairs of bats came to live in the cave. They heard them fly. They watched them sleep, upside down. Eve lost her compulsion to draw. Exhausted from their attempt to survive, they prepared to die.

"We must not fear death anymore," she said. "That may be why the animals are happy, Adam, because they don't fear it."

"Maybe we never were eternal. Perhaps we simply weren't aware that we would die. Maybe that was Paradise," he said.

Eve wept. She wept easily now. She thought that weeping would lighten the water in her stomach. Adam embraced her. His arms did not completely reach around her anymore and he was afraid that if he entered her he would be caught by the creature that lived in her belly, but he cuddled her against his chest. Sleeping was a relief. The gray, dull days blended into moonlit nights. The more they slept, the more they wanted to sleep. They barely woke to slake their thirst, urinate, and relieve their bowels. Numb with cold, Adam would look out of the mouth of the cave and wonder if the stars were the luminous sands of a dark sea on the other side of the sky they would finally sink into.

They were startled from dreams in which they were always dying, tumbling down precipices or failing in their attempt to return to the Garden, by the sound of the downpour they heard through the opening of the cave.

Eve felt the warm breeze. She opened her eyes. She looked at Adam, sleeping listlessly, with his arm over his face. She touched her belly to be sure that it wasn't her internal sea that was overflowing. She sat on a stone and watched the water streaming down outside in transparent, shining threads. She shook Adam.

"It's raining. It's raining," she exclaimed in a tone of celebration. She was sure that now they would not die of the cold.

They had survived their first winter.

CHAPTER 17

*A*DAM AND EVE BATHED IN THE RAIN. THEY WERE thin. They looked at each other and pointed to their bones. They laughed. The cold water washed away the sandy crust in their eyelashes, the dust, the rancid odor. Eve looked at him and knew that he was thinking the same thing she was, remembering the moment when he knew he had come to be, and also when she woke at his side and they realized they were man and woman. They had never talked about that, but they had a way of looking at each other in which they recognized the presence of that memory. They dried themselves in the sun. They had regained the upright walk and happy gaze of their earliest existence. Adam wondered how many days it might have rained while they dreamed they were dying, because the world was once again green and opulent. As soon as the rain stopped, the clouds were dragged away by the wind, and above them the sky was intensely blue, with the splendor of a sunny day.

Eve used Adam's help in getting over puddles the water had

left like shining eyes on the earth. Not only had the land recovered from the cold, the branches of the fig tree that had
been left blackened by the fire had sprouted new leaves that
showed no trace of the damage. The tree was bursting with fat,
juicy figs. They cut them and sat down to eat. The fruit had
the flavor of their last day in the Garden of Eden, and also of
their first intimacy. Adam put aside his ephemeral rancor as he
recalled Eve's delicate, perfect hand holding out the forbidden
fruit. Their tenacious nostalgia gave way before their relief at
being alive and seeing the colors of the world recover their
intensity.

Adam helped Eve climb a section of mountain from which
they looked out over a large number of animals placidly grazing on the grass again growing on the plain. Eve pointed out
goats, horses, deer, antelope, sheep. There were identical, but
much smaller, creatures beside them, gamboling and nibbling
grass.

"Your time is coming soon." The Serpent was coiled around
the branch of a thorny bush.

"You!" Eve exclaimed.

"I slept all winter. A long sleep. A lot of wasted time."

"Will the cold come again?"

"As punctual as hunger, but before that the plants will grow
again and it will be very hot. Winter comes after the leaves fall."

"What time are you saying will come for me?"

"You can't guess?"

"What will come out of me?"

"Twins, Eve. Male and female. Son, daughter. That is what
your offspring, the ones that will follow you, your descendants,
will be called."

"Sons, daughters," Eve repeated.

"When will they come?" Adam asked.

"Very soon."

"How will that be?"

"With pain."

Eve looked at the Serpent with irritation. More pain? Hadn't it been enough to see what they had already suffered from hunger and cold?

"I'm sorry, Eve. I thought I should warn you about it. That is how Elokim arranged it. I do not know why he has a certain affinity for pain. Maybe he would like to feel it. He must think that the pain of the body is easier to bear."

"Do you imagine him suffering?"

"I think that he wouldn't have created what he doesn't know."

"Maybe he imagined it. Maybe that's why he can't gauge the suffering of others."

"Don't get upset. It isn't good for you. I will go. It wasn't my intention to ruin your spring."

Her long, golden body glided along the ground; she slipped beneath some rocks and disappeared.

Adam felt like an intruder in Eve's affliction. Standing beneath the wide, luminous sky, he found it difficult to think about pain. It would be best not to think about that, he told Eve. If the animals had young, there was no reason why it would be more difficult for her.

"I am not an animal, Adam."

"Precisely," he agreed, conciliatory. "You will do it better than they."

Eve did not want to think about pain. They descended

from the foothills of the mountain and slowly walked to the river. They wandered along the bank beneath the tender green of new leaves. They sneezed from the invisible pollen floating in the air. Wild yellow, purple, and orange flowers poked their heads up among the grasses. Everything smelled of roots, of sated earth, and the air was filled with the sudden flutter of butterfly wings and the sustained song of insects that unexpectedly sprang from the undergrowth. Who understood Elokim? Adam thought. The land to which he had exiled them had a Garden beneath its skin. The so suddenly abundant green filled his eyes with tears.

Sated with seeing, hearing, and smelling the unfolding of the life they had given up for dead, they started back toward the cave. A sharp moaning sound came from some nearby clumps of brush. Eve parted the branches. On the grass, with her hooves pawing the air, lay a mare twisting with pain. Eve noted that the mare's belly was as swollen as her own, and that her sex was inflamed.

"I have to see what she's doing, Adam. I think her time has come."

Cautiously, Eve went closer. She knelt beside her. The mare made some movement as if to get up, but nearly immediately fell back. Eve moved her hands delicately in order not to frighten the mare, and ran her fingers lightly over the surface of the large belly. The stretched, taut skin, mysteriously grainy and mineral, was like hers when it contracted. With her right hand she stroked the mare's long muzzle. The horse's eyes were enormous, frightened. Eve kept passing her hand over the distended belly, the muzzle, the hair on the tight cheeks, repeating the sounds she used to soothe Adam.

Adam was contemplating the mysterious lunar outlines of the woman and the curved elevation of the mare's belly. Animal and woman stared into each other's eyes; Eve's long black hair framed her tilted head.

What do they know that I don't know? Adam thought. He felt the same reverence he experienced when he saw the Tree of Life for the first time.

Man and woman held their breath when two small extremities appeared in the sex of the mare. A moment later, after a painful whinny, the mare expelled a tiny foal, perfect, made in her image and likeness. Enclosed in a white, bloody membrane, the miniature horse lay on the weeds. Neither Adam nor Eve dared touch it. An hour passed. The mare broke the foal's wrapping with her teeth. The little creature made an attempt to stand on its feet. It fell and got up several times before it succeeded. Huffing, the mare, she too standing now, conscientiously began to clean her foal.

Eve touched her roundness. Air escaped from her lungs with a sigh of relief and amazement. That was how it was, she thought. Adam was right. If the animals could do it, she would do it better.

CHAPTER 18

*E*VE BARELY SLEPT THAT NIGHT, IMAGINING THE TINY offspring the Serpent had announced to her. She laughed quietly, not to wake Adam, thinking how in her early imaginings, and then his, she had populated her inner self with fish, dolphins, and even marine monsters. She encircled her belly with her arms. She thought of her small, moist sex as a fleshy mollusk. She shivered. Maybe everything would have to tear apart. She closed her eyes tight to calm her sudden fearful agitation. The mare had got to her feet after her labor. She would do the same. She refused to think of the pain. She tried to imagine her daughter and her son. Would they be like her and Adam? Or would they be different, as she and Adam were different from Elokim? She rubbed her hand over her taut, round stomach. She waited. She felt the watery movement, the light bumpings. They were there, just as she had been on Adam's rib. But he would not give birth again. Why her now? Why was she the one who would populate the solitude in which they lived? And living, was that a privilege or a punishment? Why was Elokim making her the accomplice in his creation?

What will the little ones be like? When will I know them? When will they let themselves be seen? What, exactly, will happen? How will they announce their coming? How will I know the day it will happen? Which of them will come out first? What will come out first, the feet, the hands, the head?

The next day Eve besieged Adam with questions. What could he tell her? he answered. He could barely grasp in his own imagination what was going to happen. Thinking that their young would come out the way the foal did from the mare triggered an involuntary contraction in his groin. He would rather think that the creatures would appear one morning beside them, just as Eve had appeared beside him. Eve was convinced that it wouldn't happen that way.

"It will be with pain. That is what the Serpent told me. Maybe my skin will split apart. Maybe my stomach will break open like an egg. Or maybe they will emerge from my abdomen like flowers." She was amused to see Adam's bewilderment.

Clumsy and heavy, she went outside in the afternoons. In the branches of the fig tree she found the nest of a pair of thrushes and watched them bring back insects and worms in their beaks to feed the scantily feathered chicks. Standing behind a tree on the bank of the river, she watched sheep, bison, goats, and donkeys bring their young to know the water. She thought she could see the herds and swarms of insects increasing in number; she was deafened by the hubbub of life frenetically reproducing itself. Little by little she closed into herself. She kept silent, thinking that she would hear the voice of the beings inside her announcing that their time had come.

Adam stitched together several rabbit skins, and every night he put them beside Eve in case the little things should appear at her side.

Not much time passed. It was early morning. Eve got up to urinate, and as she did a flow of water spilled down her legs. She was disturbed. Had she been mistaken and was it after all a sea inside her? She was afraid she might find herself surrounded by fish, but in the shadows that radiated from the light of the fire she did not see a fish, not any marine creature.

She went back to lie by Adam. She did not wake him until a little later.

"It hurts, Adam. The way it did when I bled."

He was quickly awake. The luminous breath of dawn was visible at the cave entrance. Eve paced back and forth, holding her lower abdomen with both hands.

"What do we do now?" Adam asked.

"I am the cave. They will come from there. You have to be on the other side so they won't drop on the stones of the floor and be hurt."

"Do you think they will like living outside the Garden?"

"I suppose that since they don't know the Garden, they will never miss it," she said, without interrupting her pacing.

"Don't you think they will remember everything we remember? They are our reflection."

"We don't remember Elokim's memories."

"No."

"Only that his memory may have been the voice we've

heard. Sometimes I think that the impetus we have to do things with our hands comes from him."

Eve suddenly panted. She stopped. She bent over.

"Adam, they're biting me!"

Just then, pain filled her completely. Adam helped her down to the stone where they slept, but Eve did not want to be lying down. She slipped to where she could prop her back against some rocks. The pain had lessened.

"I thought they were eating me." Eve smiled, bathed in sweat.

But she thought the same thing a while later, and then again. The pain came and went. "It's a bit like the sea," she told Adam. "It moves in waves. Every wave pulls something from me; maybe the son and the daughter are connected to my flesh, and Elokim is using a sharpened stone to get them out."

The pain grew stronger. The explanations she had come up with as she tried to understand what was happening to her body came to an end. Instead of reasoning, she began to resist ferociously, gritting her teeth, drawing up, protectively embracing her abdomen, crying and yelling at the top of her lungs. Behind her, patting her head, stroking her hair, Adam was crying and yelling, too. The bats, of which there were now many, woke from their daytime sleep and flew to the highest part of the cave. The tone of the screams, the man's and the woman's weeping, swelled in proportion to the increasing pressure of the clenched fist Eve feared would end by crushing her. Her cries were far-reaching, unrestrained sounds repeated by the cave and sent out to the world through the opening that served as a skylight. Adam's were hoarse, bewildered howls of impotence and rage. Every part of his body was filled with the woman's pain. He wept inconsolably as he watched her suffer.

The wind carried Adam's and Eve's cries to the great plain, where animals were grazing, spread them through the mountains, lowered them onto the river. Golden and feline beasts, horses, foxes, rabbits, the bear, the lizard, the partridge, cows, goats, the buffalo of the plain, the monkeys; animals of every species and size began to follow the lament as if it were a summons. Clouds of dust rose beneath the hooves of the horses, the swift paws of the tigers, the bears and bison, as if the wordless sound had penetrated the forgetfulness that had possessed them when they left the Garden. Falcons, eagles, doves, blackbirds, woodpeckers, and bluebirds were the first to enter and light on rocks projecting from the walls of the cave, now covered with Eve's drawings. Little by little, all through that day crisscrossed with laments, large quadrupeds, the donkeys, the coyotes, the wolves came in silently. Adam had a moment of panic when he saw tigers, boars, and leopards cross the threshold of the cave. His yells turned into moans of surprise and sobs of relief and awe when he saw horses, goats, and deer file in one after the other; hunter and prey suddenly free of the hunger and the instinct that made them enemies. Leaning against the stone, sunk in her pain, with her head between her knees, rocking back and forth, Eve sensed them before she saw them; she felt enveloped in a warm breath, in a dense, gentle air that softened the space that surrounded and sustained her. She looked up and saw the animals pressing close in a tight circle around her with an air of reconciliation and recognition, as if nature had suddenly regressed to the time that had no surprises or death, when they had all shared the freshness and the while petals of Paradise.

A horse nudged Adam's shoulder with its muzzle, and an ocelot licked Eve's face. In all the time since Elokim had ejected them from the Garden, Eve had not felt so fully accompanied. The solid bodies of the animals, their gentle expressions, made her feel nostalgic for her own innocence. She sobbed with a strangely happy sadness. She became aware of how much she had missed the quiet simplicity of the beasts. She felt such profound gratitude and tenderness to think that her pain had moved them so that she let go of everything that was holding her back. In that emptying, she relaxed the muscles with which, by trapping his creatures in her belly, she had defiantly refused to share Elokim's creation. Surrounded by the animals, looking into Adam's expression of awe and wonderment, she made a supreme effort, and screamed with all her might; and it was thus that the first woman brought forth her children to live upon the Earth.

CHAPTER 19

*A*N ENORMOUS YELLOW MOON WAS FLOATED HIGH in the night. Adam cut his daughter's and his son's umbilical cords. The eagle and the falcon carried off one of the placentas; the other was eaten by a small tiger and a nanny goat. The scent of blood shattered the quiet. Low growls followed, and the most vulnerable animals hastily scurried away. The fiercest slunk from the cave, dazed, with the stunned expression of having been wakened from a dream, not knowing where they were. In the cave the only animals left were the dog, the cat, and the bats hanging upside down overhead.

Adam and Eve wept as they watched the animals leave. They continued to weep, unable to control their tears, a noiseless, unending stream, the overflow of accumulated emotions. They were never to forget that rare and ineffable event.

At last they came back to reality. Adam watched Eve fall in and out of sleep. She was having trouble resting. Her wish to closely inspect the tiny, naked little bodies that Adam had laid beside her kept her awake. He was looking at them, too, but was unable to concentrate. He was thinking about the animals. My animals, he kept telling himself. My animals came back. How lonely I have been without them! They are mine, but they came for her, for that pain I was not allowed to share.

The tiny beings moved their hands, their feet. From time to time they started, as if they were having nightmares. They opened their eyes a bit and closed them again. Adam lay down beside the skin where the little ones were. At last, Eve went to sleep. He tucked his toes between hers and he too fell asleep.

Eve woke many times during the night. She had stopped crying. Her body hurt, but the pain was tolerable, mild. How I yelled, she thought. Everything I didn't know how to say I shouted to the air. She regretted that it had occurred to her to block the twins' way out when she was furious about the pain Elokim had arranged for her. Only the arrival of the animals had managed to dissolve her rancor and washed it away from her heart.

It was early morning when Adam opened his eyes. Eve smiled at him. The man and the woman looked at the son and the daughter.

"They are different from us," said Adam. "I doubt they can walk."

"Maybe in a few days," said Eve. "The foal did."

"And what will they eat?"

Eve looked at their faces. She leaned closer. She looked inside their mouths.

"Adam, they have no teeth!"

"The foal and the calf are eating from their mother's teats."

Eve touched her breasts. They hurt. They were large, and swollen. She lay back and closed her eyes. What did Adam expect? That her body not only make the offspring but also feed them? She was so tired. Her time had already come and passed. Now she wanted to sleep for days, regain her strength, feel that her body belonged to her again. The little ones began to cry. Their wailing pierced her skin, as if it were inside of her. She lay still, with her eyes closed. It was a sad sound, frail, helpless.

"They're hungry, Eve," Adam said. "Give them whatever that is that comes from your breasts."

"Why don't you do it, Adam? You have nipples, too."

Adam looked at her, not knowing what to think. He picked up one of the twins. Eve watched as the little thing searched for its father's breast. She got up. It hurt to walk but she went outside the cave to escape the wailing. Adam called her. "Eve, Eve, where are you going?" but she didn't answer, and she didn't turn back. She wanted to sleep, rest. She sank down beneath the shade of one of the fig trees. She rested her back against the trunk of the tree. She could barely hear the wailing of the twins. She closed her eyes. Straight overhead, from the center of the sky, the sun was illuminating a blue springtime. Her consciousness wound into a black ball and rolled toward the quiet of sleep

"This isn't the time for sleep, Eve; wake up."

She felt the cold body of the Serpent brush her arm. When she was able to pull herself out of the heavy sleep in which she had taken refuge, she was quickly alert. She saw the reptile's tail coiled around a low branch, her head floating in the air close by.

"You had to wake me up."

"I couldn't miss this event. You have made a man and a woman for Elokim."

"It hurt a lot."

"Have you noticed that animals walk on four feet?"

"You drag yourself along."

"Leave me out of this for the moment. You do not have the large body of a mare or a cow. You walk upright. That is why the young of your species will be born small and helpless. You will have to give them food, take care of them until they're grown."

"And you, like Adam, are going to tell me that I have to give them what comes out of my breasts."

"When he took you two from the Garden, Elokim reversed the direction of time. In the Garden you were eternal. You would never have had children. It wasn't necessary for you to reproduce, since you would never have died. Now reality must be re-created. Creation must return to the point where it can begin again."

"I don't understand."

"Your children, Eve, your children will return time to its beginnings. You must feed them."

"My children will know hunger and thirst, and what about knowledge? Will they dream? Have imagination?"

"They are your reflection."

"If I was eternal and perfect, then why was I was consumed in the Garden by the desire to know? It doesn't make sense."

"You are very perceptive," the Serpent said with irony. "Eternity does not require knowledge. For life and survival, that knowledge becomes indispensable. Questions must be answered. Yet in the absence of uncertainty, fear, knowledge becomes irrelevant. If one is happy, if one lacks for nothing, why is knowledge necessary? Abundance is permanent. But perhaps you were nostalgic."

"Nostalgic? I didn't know any other life. It was you who told me there was another way to live."

"It's possible to feel nostalgia for what one has never lived. Maybe Elokim instilled nostalgia in you so you would eat the fruit."

"I no longer know what I think. I don't understand why he did it."

"He gets bored, I told you. Imagine how entertaining it can be to create a creature in your image and likeness, give it nothing except knowledge, give it a world, and then wait to see if it is capable of returning to the perfect point of departure."

"And you were his accomplice?"

"I was not aware of things I know now. He has explained them since to mortify me. I have also been punished. He has made me regress farther than you and Adam. Look how I have to crawl. Future generations will blame you, but as your descendents acquire more knowledge, you will regain your prestige. In contrast, no one will be the advocate for a pitiful serpent. I will be made the incarnation of evil."

"I'm sorry," said Eve.

"I thought that it wouldn't be long before Elokim took me out of this ridiculous disguise, but his rage has not yet ebbed."

"It could be that he suffers more than we imagine."

"He knows too much. Knowledge and suffering are inseparable. I should be going," she said, sliding down the trunk of the tree. "You go and tend to your young. Yield to your animal instinct. No one is better equipped than you to do it," she muttered sarcastically, disappearing into the undergrowth.

On the way back to the cave, Eve heard the twins yelling so loudly that she thought she would find them already grown. She walked faster. When she got there, Adam held one of them up, listless, its head lolling.

"Let me try," said Eve. She held it in the crook of her arm. It was the girl child. Eyes closed, her face bright red, she was screaming at the top of her lungs. As soon as the heat of the little body burrowed against her side, the milk in Eve's breasts flowed like water from a spring. Stunned, she took the child's head and guided the tiny mouth to her nipple.

"Give me the other one, Adam. Be careful. Put your hand beneath its head."

Eve sat down on the rock. The girl sucked ravenously. Tickles ran down Eve's spine. Adam laid the boy child in her other arm. He squatted behind Eve so that she could lean against his legs. At last there was silence. Adam drew a breath of relief.

"I met the Serpent out there. She says our children will be helpless. We will have to care for them until they are grown," she murmured.

"A long time?"

"She didn't say."

"It's strange," said Adam. "You're doing what animals do, but you're not at all like them."

"Yes, I am like them, but it doesn't matter. It's what we are now. Did you see how my milk began to flow when I felt their hunger? As if my body knew to obey them. And they are so small. Look at them. Arrogance is useless."

"Is that what the Serpent told you?"

"Something like that. She doesn't fully comprehend what's happened, either. She likes to pretend she knows, but it's difficult to decipher what she says."

The girl's eyes were open. They were gray. She was covered in a whitish, greasy substance; her features astonishingly fine and perfect. The skin and hair of the boy were darker. His eyes were also gray. Without gills or scales, how could they have survived so many months floating in the thick water of her womb? Such mystery! she thought.

After the twins had their fill, Eve asked Adam to wash them. He did so with care, so as not to frighten them. The little female had lighter hair; the boy's eyes were fixed on him. He washed the tiny hands, the feet, the minute buttocks. He cleaned their faces, examined their diminutive ears, their nostrils. He put a finger into each mouth, felt each tongue.

Eve watched him, curious and amused. She felt filled to the brim with milk; filled were her breasts, her heart.

"We must give them a name," she said.

What would she and Adam be like if they had been born so small? she wondered. No one had ever washed them, or looked on them with eyes so moist, so gentle.

CHAPTER 20

THE NEXT DAY IT WAS RAINING LIGHTLY. ADAM LEFT the cave, accompanied by his dog, Cain. He could not stop pondering the mystery of the little creatures that had emerged from the dark tunnel in which he had more than once thought he would disappear. Eve trembled when she reached her innermost laughter. For him, to capture that trembling was to breathe again the air of the Garden of Eden. Now he wondered if instead he would remember the pain he had seen in her face, as her body shook and squeezed to expel the fruit of the seed he probably had helped grow, watering it with the liquid that came from his penis. But trees never wept at birth. Plants surged silently from the ground. In contrast, life had burst from her like a cataclysm. He didn't bleed, his body didn't change, and nothing about the birth had hurt him physically. Why not? Why only Eve? What did it mean?

He walked down to the river with the intention of throwing out his net to catch some fish.

The wet earth shook its back, scattering water in thin streamers that formed small deltas in the reddish mud. Cain and Adam moved with sure steps, hopping among the puddles, breathing in the intense scents. Suddenly Cain stopped. He pricked his ears and growled. Through the underbrush, Adam glimpsed a small bear, a cub looking at them with curiosity. He scolded Cain. After seeing the animals surround Eve, he had imagined that things would again be like the days in the Garden. He was concerned about the small animals he would still need to hunt, but he had convinced himself that they were there because they were destined to serve as food. He moved toward the cub, paternal, friendly, soothing voice. The cub did not move. Adam was about to reach out and pat its head when he heard the sound of a large animal crashing toward him in an uproar of branches and leaves. The mother bear was racing toward him. Confounded by the sudden return to distrust and aggression, Adam leaped to the nearest tree and began to climb, terrified. Grunting, infuriated, the bear followed. Adam felt its claws rip the soles of his feet. His skin ached and so did his heart. Jumping in to defend him, Cain attacked the bear from the side. The dog was strong, short muzzle, solid, rounded head. Surprised, annoyed by the interruption, the bear slapped the dog into the brush with one paw. Cain attacked again. The bear stopped. From the tree, Adam shouted, "Careful, Cain; leave it, Cain." The dog was nipping at the bear's legs and claws, unable now to go against instinct and retire. The enormous animal, enraged, fell upon the dog. The last thing Adam saw was Cain's neck in the jaws of the bear, as it jerked him from side to side. Cain's growls turned into sharp yelps of pain; a long, sad, horrifying moan was the final sound Adam heard before the bear dropped the lifeless body of the dog at its feet and lifted its eyes toward the branch where he was crouching.

The man was not sure how he killed the bear. He remembered the beast's odor, its claws red from Cain's fresh blood, its monstrous strength, and he also remembered the infinite power of his rage, the rock he had used to crush the bear's face, eyes, and snout.

He was bleeding. He was clawed, bitten, but alive. Nothing that wouldn't heal. On the other hand, Cain lay on the ground, the loyal, alert gaze now gone from his staring eyes. Adam came to himself. He did not know what beast he had turned into. A beast capable of killing a bear with his bare hands. His body shook as if lashed by a gale. He knelt. He touched the dog's forehead, his ears. He was cold, limp, his head swinging from his trunk. Adam picked him up and clasped him to his breast. He had seen the remains of other animals, what the tigers and lions left. When he saw them, he thought of nothing but eating them. He never gave a thought to how they had died, or what kind of lives they had lived. There, with his dead dog, he thought of all those things. Death was always the same, but his dog was different. He knew Adam. He knew what Adam was thinking. He protected him. He licked his hands, curled up beside him and warmed him at night. He was distinct. Adam slipped to the ground with his dog. He remembered him playing. He wept. He covered his face with his hands and let loose his grief.

He buried Cain. He skinned the bear. He went to the river and washed off the blood. He went back to the cave.

"I know what we will name the boy," he told Eve. "We will call him Cain."

Eve did not like what she saw in the man's face. She had loved the dog, too. She cried over him. She would miss him, but she didn't like the sound of the name Cain when Adam said it would be the boy's.

"I think we should give the boy a different name."

"No, it's a good name."

"But that one will always make you sad."

"I will get over it."

"You killed the bear," said Eve. "You brought back its skin. It frightens me. Such a huge animal. I didn't think it was possible."

"Nor I. And I can't explain how I did it. I could have done anything."

"It enraged you and you punished it."

"Yes."

"Elokim also condemned us to die."

Death. His lifeless dog. The dry snout. The opaque eyes. The lolling head. When Adam buried him, he was cold, stiff. In one instant, everything that had been Cain had disappeared. What remained of the dog now existed only in him, in Eve, and in the drawings on the walls of the cave. They were dust and unto dust they would return. Would others someday know where on Earth Eve and he had been laid to rest, where their recently born children? Who would remember them? How would anyone remember them? He recalled his dream about the trees with human heads, how they broke away and fell. It made little difference that more and more men and women would be born to life. They would all die. One after the other. The dry snout and opaque eyes. Cold. Stiff. Like Cain. And yet every day they would feel the hunger, the anxiety to survive. He was amazed to see how avid the twins were at Eve's breast. Such desire to live in every animal, every plant, as if death didn't matter, as if it were not real.

His rage developed into a fever that lodged in his groin. Eve's body radiated the brightness of the milk that flowed from her breasts. In the darkness of the cave, asleep with the children on the black bearskin, her skin glowed, reflecting the golds and oranges of the fire and revealing a new, inviting roundness. She held back his impulse until she no longer feared he could hurt her inside. Then she celebrated with him the novelty of her waist, recovered from the sea. At night, when their bodies came together, Adam often remembered the strength that had destroyed the bear, and he feared his hands on the woman's delicate bones. In addition to setting the lines of her body more firmly, maternity had brought her the awareness of a power in her that was beyond physical strength. She knew that Adam perceived it, and that this was why he never tired of searching her inner being, and seeking refuge in her dark, moist shelter.

So it was that not very much time went by between the birth of the twins and Eve's premonition that she was hosting new creatures. The waves of another sea were swishing within her. She remembered that the Serpent had told her the experience would be repeated. Although it was not her will, she thought that the body must have its reasons. This time, unlike the first time, she was not afraid. The pain had soon been forgotten. It had been erased by the amazement of seeing those frail beings beginning to become themselves, and by the enigma of how they could be so unpredictable and yet so strangely a part of her. Their wailing, their hunger, and their cold were a part of her. And yet no part of her had been lost. Lying with the children as they nursed, she often found peace. Sky, river, Nature folding and unfolding before her eyes, the night and its myriad lights, the mysteriously enclosed sea, the sun, moon, trees, animals, all contained a happiness that because it was so tenuous and threatened was not abundant. To see her young ones react to her counsel and caresses and recognize her, to see the jubilation in their eyes and their little hands when she came near, made it increasingly difficult to think of herself as the victim of an arbitrary and disproportionate punishment.

Part 2

GO FORTH
AND MULTIPLY

CHAPTER 21

*A*DAM LOOKED AT THE CUTS ON THE TREES. THERE were many now. The bark on nearly all the trees along the path from the cave to the river was scarred with slashes. He did not know how to count, but it was enough to look at all those wounded trees to know that this land they were living in was consuming his life with every cut. As if that were not enough, time's passing was marked on the bodies of their children. That was how Eve counted the days: watching them grow.

And now they were grown, although they were not yet mature. Abel and Aklia were newer than Cain and Luluwa, but the difference was imperceptible. The time it took for the four to walk, talk, and fend for themselves seemed interminable while it lasted, but now Adam missed it. It had not been easy to teach them the ways of life. None of them had been able to walk without first crawling on his or her knees. Attempting to stand, they fell and bruised themselves. None of them seemed aware of what could happen to them in rocky places, or near the cliffs. He and Eve had to lead them by the hand. He remembered how their backs used to hurt after bending over all day to prop them up as they took their first steps. They could not take their eyes off the children for a minute. What the children lacked in dexterity they more than made up for in curiosity. They were like their mother. They wanted to touch everything, but they didn't know that fire burned and that it was easy to harm themselves. Eve said that this was because they had no knowledge of Good and Evil. She gave them figs to eat, but these had no great effect. Adam could not understand why the children were so ignorant. He tended to believe that since Eve and he shared characteristics with animals, it was possible that their children resembled animals even more than they did. The cat, however, never dirtied the cave with its excrement, but the little ones urinated or defecated wherever they felt like it. Only after a tenacious struggle did they learn that that they were supposed to go outside, and always cover their excrement with dirt. They had begun to seem more alert only when they started to talk. At first it was difficult to understand them. Before their brothers, Aklia and Luluwa were able to say what they wanted. It was a time of laughter for Eve and Adam. They split their sides as they listened to their children's words for water, cat, breast. But later, when all four were spilling over with talk, they realized how different each was from the others. They learned that they could teach the children how to live but could not domesticate them.

Eve's fear of winter, and her fear that her milk would not be enough to feed the four, was the goad that transformed her intuition concerning the Earth and its fruits into sound knowledge. Around the cave were growing almond and pear trees, grapevines, wheat, oats, and edible roots. Cain and Luluwa had inherited their mother's skill at identifying vegetables and herbs. It was they who tended the garden, while Abel, who from the time he was small had demonstrated a knowledge of animals, had domesticated nanny goats for milk, and sheep whose wool Aklia wove so that they could clothe themselves without having to kill.

Eve did not feel nostalgic about the twins' early years. She did not, like Adam, lament how swiftly they had grown. He said that it seemed he could still see them when they had just dared to stand on their own, how they used to stumble and plop down, how he had looked at them half amused, half frightened. Eve treasured those tender images but she was happier now that they looked after themselves. She had not forgotten the consuming fatigue of the time when the children had not let them draw a breath, always clinging to them possessively. While she and Adam were learning to cultivate the land and to provide themselves with shelter and food—so that Adam did not have to go out and leave her alone with the impossible task of looking after four tiny, defenseless beings—they had lived the lives of herd animals, moving from place to place with the children straddling their hips. The first winters they'd had to shelter in the cave, for days and nights living in a world of babbling in which words resolved nothing and instinct was their only sure guide. Adam tolerated the change of routine better than she, but he abandoned his long explorations and hunts because the thought that something might have happened to them always made him race back. He came to the conclusion that it was better to be hungry together than to take the risk that the dangers of the world might keep them apart. For Eve it was difficult to adapt to seeing her body converted into a source of food for four pairs of eyes that required her to lie down and offer her breasts. Ashamed of her own emotions, she never confessed to Adam that she had often wanted to escape, to run away from them. Ever since he had witnessed the birth and learned that her body was capable not only of creating children but also of feeding them, he had considered her a marvel. Elokim had given her so much power, Adam said, that by making her suffer blood and pain he probably thought he would prevent her from defying him. Eve did not contradict Adam's interpretation. She admired Adam's gentle tenacity, the dedication with which he applied himself to the tasks he was constantly creating for himself, the satisfaction he received from controlling and understanding the world about him. He was willful, however, and persisted in doing what he wanted without regard for the effect his action might eventually have. It was difficult for him to be patient, to observe the natural course of events, to let them develop according to their inclination or wisdom. He was always in a hurry. For that reason, although he understood the cycle of the fruits of the earth, he preferred hunting, the immediate, the things that brought the swiftest rewards for his efforts.

Eve, on the other hand, perceived what happened around her as if she were able to see through more eyes than her own. It was no effort for her to hear inside herself what others might be thinking. In the time it took her children to reach adolescence, it seemed to her that her skin had grown ears and that her eyes had developed a tactile sense that allowed her to perceive the narrowness or intensity of her children's feelings. She read their attitudes and gestures with a skill that often surprised her. To have come out of herself, to have multiplied, had mysteriously opened for her the secret languages of life. She intuited even the humor of plants and trees and sky. Even so, she could not figure out whether, like her, her children possessed the knowledge of Good and Evil; whether they would lose their innocence without eating the forbidden fruit; or whether, innocents that they were, they would learn to exist in the world of unanswered questions in which in order to eat and survive, it was necessary to kill.

In the life they'd settled into, Abel and Adam were inseparable. The same was true of Cain and Luluwa. Eve spent most of her time with little Aklia. When Aklia was born, Adam had wept when he saw her. The births had been quick and without event or portent. She and Adam were alone, confident in what they knew. It seemed less painful to Eve. That may have been because she knew what to expect and was prepared to suffer. Abel was the first to appear. Darker than Cain, larger. Strong lungs, open eyes. After a long pause the pain returned. Eve expelled Aklia, a tiny little creature, eyes tightly closed, face covered with dark fuzz, round forehead, lips too large. Adam cut both cords. He wrapped the creatures in soft foxtails. Adam walked Aklia around the cave. He took her over to the fire. He looked at her and said that she looked like a monkey, not a human being. Aklia shed the facial hair shortly after birth, but the small face; the features grouped together in its center, below heavy eyebrows; the broad, prominent mouth; the sparse, limp hair, black as wet wood, remained. Her eyes were beautiful, however, small but shining. Aklia also had the most perfect hands and feet of all their children. She was clever and skillful.

She knew intuitively what use things could have. She made
needles from bone, she stitched skins, she wove the sheep's
wool. Her agility and small size were an advantage. No one
could equal her in climbing trees, bringing dates from the tops
of the palms. Eve protected her and spoiled her to compensate
to some degree for the inequality of the gifts she had been
allotted at birth. Although her siblings were larger and more
handsome, to Eve Aklia seemed stronger, and closer to the essence of all things around them.

For some time she and Adam had been asking themselves
what Elokim's reasons were for having Eve give birth to two
pairs of twins. Go forth and multiply, he had said, and there was
no one besides them in the world. Cain would pair with Aklia
and Abel with Luluwa, said Adam. In that way the blood of
the two births would be mingled. It was not good that blood
shared in one womb should mix. Elokim had told him that in
a dream in which Adam had seen himself again in the Garden.
A confusing dream, he said. The Garden looked old and ruined.
He could barely walk around because of the mud and all the
tree trunks lying on the ground. A moist, whitish vapor floated
among the branches of the gigantic trees from which pale
ferns streamed like tousled hair. Climbing vines with enormous toothed leaves were choking out the big cedars, and light
barely filtered through the patches of open sky in the middle
of that vegetal, swampy chaos in which species were crowded
together and entangled in what seemed a mortal struggle. In
the middle of his aimless walk, Adam saw Aklia crossing from
branch to branch, followed by a gorilla with painfully sad eyes.
He saw Cain following her, trying to topple tree after tree as
she escaped the club he was using to hack at the limbs and

trunks. He saw Abel sleeping, and Luluwa sitting beside him with her hands over her face. He spoke to his children; he ordered them to go home, but they did not hear him. They were very close, but it was if they were far away. Then, to his terror, the gorilla had spoken with the voice of Elokim: "Abel with Luluwa, Cain with Aklia. Bloods must not be mixed," he had thundered. Adam had awakened with the sound of those words echoing through the morning light.

The dream had been repeated many times since the children were small. It was a terrible dream, he told Eve, a dream that suffocated him. He always awoke with anguish, but because it persisted, he considered it a clear sign of Elokim's will.

Eve feared the compassion Aklia stirred in Adam. He treated her with condescension. She often caught him looking at his daughter with a trace of disbelief on his face, as if it was difficult for him to accept that she had appeared to them in the same way the others had. That the twins were destined to choose partners had seemed natural to Eve, especially when she considered that had females not been born, it would have fallen to her to reproduce with her own sons. A terrible world it was, she often thought. Terrible, too, the uncertainty of their lives, all the things they didn't know, despite the punishment they had suffered to achieve knowledge. How could she not imagine Elokim mocking them? Cruel Elokim. Cruel father who abandoned his creatures. Now that she was a mother, his attitude seemed even more incomprehensible. And maternity never ended. Nor did the pain. Her children were adolescents now. Soon they would have to pair off. Since she knew Adam's dreams and the plan they carried with them, she intuited as they were growing that there would be no way to prevent their

suffering. Cain had been strong from the time he was a boy—
and stoic. He hurt himself and only rarely cried, as if from a
tender age he harbored the consciousness of an adult patiently
waiting for his body to mature. For him Luluwa, beautiful
Luluwa, was the beginning and end of happiness. Eve saw them
as the two sides of a being that existed only when they were
together. Both were quiet, gruff with the others but warm and
pleasant with each other. They had the gift of understanding each other on the strength of a look. Luluwa's increasing
beauty, which was perturbing Abel, and even Adam, was for
Cain as natural and uplifting as the flowering of a tree preparing to give fruit. That he saw her with such transparency did
not, however, mean that he was indifferent to her beauty. Quite
the opposite—it made him happy because he was sure that
Luluwa was his partner, and that he would always be with her.

"Are you sure, Adam, that Elokim said that bloods should
not be mixed? The animals do."

"You know very well that we are not like them."

He could not go against the dreams, he said. Eve was tormented by the possibility that the dream was a reflection of
Adam's preference for Abel. The gift Abel had for commu-
nicating with animals reminded Adam of the way they had
obeyed him in the Garden of Eden. Abel was handsome, like
Luluwa. Taller than his father, with coppery skin. His face with
its long, straight nose and high cheekbones was striking, and
his eyes, like those of his sister, were the shade of the light-
colored leaves on the Tree of Life. Cain was not as tall. His features were not as well set as his brother's, but they were agreeable,
even handsome. Nevertheless, perhaps because he had since he
was a boy felt that his fondness for the land, and his silent ways,

had disappointed his father, Cain had turned into an unsociable, sober boy. His shoulders slumped when he walked. When his father spoke to him, he lowered his eyes. He undoubtedly resented the constant comparisons with Abel, and even with the clever and faithful dog whose name he had inherited. For Eve he did tender little things that compensated for his muteness. He brought her the sweetest pears, and the fruits of his laborious efforts to multiply plants by crossbreeding and watering them from the spring by means of a ditch he had dug with his own hands. Luluwa and Cain harvested strange hybrids that Eve and Aklia tested, although more than once these hybrids had made them sick. But if Cain and Luluwa quietly appeared with their baskets of vegetables, Abel's entrances into the cave were triumphal: he brought milk from the flocks of goats that tamely followed him, he hunted deer, he herded lambs, he had trained more dogs, and had even worked out a system to make birds like the falcon share their prey with him. It was difficult to resist Abel's innocent goodness. Eve was convinced that he was not even aware of his brother's jealousy. Abel's world was simple and peaceful. He counted on the constant approval and praise of his father and the company of the animals. He spent his days smiling, exploring the jungles beyond the river, and returning at sunset with his stories. Cain resented the fact that Elokim had banished his parents from the Garden. Abel, on the other hand, wanted to get on Elokim's good side. On the stone where Adam offered to the Other the first products of the sweat of his brow, Abel also left his.

"Abel is simpler. He would be better with Aklia. She isn't beautiful, but she is in better touch with the world. She knows how to make hooks from fragments of deer bones and needles from the spines of fish. She thinks more than Luluwa does," Eve insisted.

"If you weren't so preoccupied with Cain, you would realize that it is he, and not Abel, that Aklia loves."

"She would come to love Abel. He is easy to love."

"I didn't say that she doesn't love him. But she prefers Cain."

"When do you think they will begin to look at each other the way we did after we ate of the fruit of the Tree?"

"I don't believe it will be much longer, Eve."

"Have you seen that Aklia and Luluwa already have breasts?"

"Yes. As soon as they bleed we will have to give each girl her partner."

"How I fear that day, Adam."

CHAPTER 22

$\mathcal{I}$T HAD BEEN A LONG TIME SINCE ADAM HAD LAID poles across the entrance to the cave to keep animals from getting in and attacking them. It could happen any day, however. There were more of them now in the cave. They stored food; they cooked it. The scent of their lives floated far away. When food became scarce and the cold returned, they would be in danger. It was time to leave and look for a new refuge. There were lots of places in the rocky formations around them, but they needed to find one with a wide entrance, one they could dig a trench in front of. That would make them inaccessible. Only they would be able to get in by walking across the tree trunks they would pull inside at night. Not a new idea, Eve said. That was how Elokim had prevented them from returning to Paradise. The abyss. They would do the same.

Aklia and Eve found a cave that suited their purpose. It was wide, with a high ceiling and an opening in the upper part where the smoke of the fire could escape.

Cain found stout limbs whose tips could be used to dig the earth, and Adam marked the size of the hole they would dig.

Cain and Luluwa were strong. Side by side, they dug in unison, giving the work their full attention. Aklia and Abel tried to imitate them. Aklia had to quit. Abel did not give up. He wanted Luluwa to see that he was as strong as Cain, thought Eve, observing them. What did Elokim have in mind by making one of her daughters so much more beautiful than the other? Why did beauty have such power? She could see them, both Abel and Adam, follow Luluwa's movements, pause on the dimples high on her hips, her long legs, her arms, her breasts. It was impossible, even for her, not to admire the limber body, straightening and bending over to dislodge the scoops of dirt. Adam was conscious that Eve was resting beneath a nearby tree. He would look at his daughter out of the corner of his eye, and then quickly look away, ashamed of what he was thinking. Abel had no villainy in mind, but he could not hide his fascination. Eve watched as Cain suddenly stopped, took Luluwa's arm, and pushed her so she was in front of him. From where she sat, Eve could see her son confront his brother, threateningly. She saw Abel, surprised, look at his father. Adam told Luluwa to take a rest beside Eve. "I'm not tired," she said. "Doesn't matter," said Adam. "Go sit with your mother."

Luluwa sat down beside Aklia, who was weaving a mat from vines. Solitary Luluwa. From the time Luluwa was very young, Eve had been aware that the air was lighter around her, like a wrap that isolated her from the others. She had been a beautiful little girl, but as she grew older beauty closed around her, setting her apart, just as the precipice had separated them from the Garden.

There was nothing in nature, nothing in insects, landscapes, plants, to evoke the bedazzlement of the heart that Luluwa stirred without doing anything more than exist. She is more beautiful than you, Adam had admitted to Eve, telling her that he had never thought any other creature could come close to her in beauty. Eve, until very recently, had thought that Luluwa, like Abel, was gifted with an absolute and noble innocence incapable of imagining the complexities that tormented the others. It was easy to take as arrogance Abel's ingenuous belief in the innate good of the world, his inalterable happiness, his surprise when faced with what the others considered incomprehensible, questionable, even perverse.

In the Garden, the Serpent had told Eve that Elokim did not want to give them knowledge because he did not want them to lose their docility; he wanted them to be like the cat and the dog. That was Abel, a handsome, sweet, docile creature—simple as a child.

But Luluwa was not like him, however much Eve wanted them to think of her in that way. Luluwa was conscious of the power of her radiance. Exercising it was part of her being, of what made her feel she was different. Eve was not sure, however, that Luluwa was entirely aware of the effect she had on her brothers, and even on Adam.

Aklia covered herself with a tunic she had woven from straw and grasses. Luluwa wore a very small skin tied around her waist.

"You need to cover yourself, Luluwa," her mother said.

"You are not a girl any longer. You disturb your brothers, and even your father."

"It isn't my fault that I am how I am," she said.

"I know that."

"How is it that I look at them and I'm not disturbed? They need to worry about themselves."

Eve fell silent. Luluwa did not often speak. When she did, it was categorical.

"Luluwa is right," said Aklia. "Why do they get disturbed and we don't?"

"You would like for Cain to be disturbed by you, isn't that true, Aklia?" said Luluwa.

"Is that true, Aklia?" her mother asked.

"I have always felt closer to Cain," said Aklia. "He is less perfect than Abel. I am less perfect than Luluwa."

"But Cain is my twin," said Luluwa. "He is mine and I am his."

"Abel never even looks at me," said Aklia. "Cain brings me fruits and nuts."

"Abel looks only at himself. He doesn't need us. He doesn't need anyone," said Luluwa.

"He is very good," said Eve. "He is happy."

"He never has doubts," said Luluwa. "He never questions what he does. He and his animals understand each other perfectly."

They were silent. The three watched the men, who were still digging.

Was it true that only the men felt aroused? Luluwa and Aklia were still very young to know, but Eve had felt the vehemence of her body when Adam cradled her in the night. It was when he was close, however, that he had this effect in her. Just looking at him wasn't enough. Yes, she believed that Adam was beautiful, and she admired the massiveness of his arms, the breadth of his chest, and the strength of his legs; but it was his eyes, the way he looked at her, that would turn day or night into the propitious moment to shelter one inside the other, and in the midst of the solitude of their banishment know the consolation of being together. It was clear that the men were definitely more impressionable. Beauty, simply by being beauty, called to their bodies. Watching them look at Luluwa, Eve saw that there was distance among them, and that they were possessed by an instinct that impelled them to quarrel over prey. How to understand that beauty disquieted them rather than instilling in them a desire to celebrate it? She would have to ask Adam, Eve thought. Abel surely would not know how to answer. Or Cain. Was it Luluwa's beauty, or could there be another reason? The sun? The moon? Where was all this going to end? What would happen when Adam told Cain that Luluwa was to be Abel's partner?

Eve had a dream about the Serpent. The Serpent appeared as she had been before she dragged herself along on the ground. She was standing beside the tree, her golden skin covered with scales, her face flat, soft feathers on her head.

"Did Elokim forgive you?" Eve asked.

"He forgives me in dreams."

"What does he dream?"

"He dreams that he has regrets. He is afraid."

"What will make us happy?"

"Restlessness. The search. Challenges."

"You said that Elokim has left us alone to test whether we

will be capable of returning to the point of departure. Only then will we be happy."

"Elokim's time is very slow."

Eve woke up. She did not want to. She closed her eyes. "When? Tell me, when will we return?" she asked in the darkness. No one answered.

CHAPTER 23

*C*ONSTRUCTING THE TRENCH TOOK THEM TWO FULL
cycles of the moon. With the second new moon, Aklia
and Luluwa bled. Eve embraced them. She calmed them.

"I don't know why it happens, but after the blood come
children."

She told each of them the story of their birth. Aklia and
Luluwa then understood what the blind hole in the middle of
their stomachs was. The navel. Neither Adam nor Eve had one.
They asked how long before they had children; what was the
man's role? Why did Abel and Cain look like Adam?

Eve smiled. They wanted to know everything.

It was early. The season of rains and cold was beginning.
The men had gone out to look for tree trunks to make the
footbridge for the trench. Eve stayed with the girls. She made
a comfortable place for them on the bear skin. She stirred the
fire. She thought about the words she would use to tell them
what they wanted to know.

She had been inside Adam before they ate of the fruit of

the Tree of Knowledge of Good and Evil, she said. Adam, instead, had never been inside her. Until they were no longer eternal, they had never felt that they needed each other. Death had forced them to seek a different kind of eternity by creating others who would keep their memories alive and be there after they were gone. Elokim had told them that dust they were and unto dust they would return. But he had also commanded them to be fruitful and multiply.

She did not know whether it would be the same for them, she continued. As for Adam and her, there came a day when she felt a profound desire to have Adam inside her. It was as if my skin could see and touch, she said. I wanted to see deep within him. I wanted to touch the air that lived within him, breathe it. I wanted to know his body and for him to know mine. I wanted another way to speak without words, that would be as clear as when the cat rubs against our legs to show his recognition. Your father felt the same way. We began by putting our lips, our tongues, together, because it is there that words have their source. We explored our saliva, our teeth, and soon we were possessed by an unknown language. It was a hot language, as if we had lighted a fire in our blood, but its words had no form. They resembled long moans, but nothing pained us. They were sighs, grunts? I don't know. Our hands filled with signs, with desires to draw unintelligible patterns on our bodies. My sex grew moist. I thought I was urinating, but it wasn't the same. Adam's penis, the thing that hangs between the legs of men, grew greatly in size. It was a hand pointed toward the center of my body. Finally we understood that that part of him had to be put into me so that we would once again be joined. It hurt when he found my moistness. I thought that he would not fit, but he did, tightly. The sensation was at first strange. We began to move. I believe Adam thought that he might touch my heart. He thrust into me as if seeking my innermost self. We rocked back and forth, like the sea on the shore. Then I felt my womb reaching out for that long hand of his, wanting to squeeze it, and wrap itself around it. When I thought I could not bear the sensation any longer, something flashed between my legs. It rose through my belly to my breasts, my arms, my head. Everything in me trembled, like the earth when thunder shakes it. Adam says that for him it was a flood, a river impetuously pouring out into me. He trembled, too, said Eve, smiling. He yelled. I think I did the same. That was all. Then we fell asleep.

We did that same thing often, once we lived outside the Garden. It has been our consolation. We gained something as we lost the eternity of the Garden. We call it love. It was while making love that Adam became mixed with you two, and with Cain and Abel. I think that is why they look like him.

Aklia and Luluwa were thoughtful. They had listened attentively. I have explained the simple part, Eve thought, fearing the question that would follow. Who will we make love with? they asked. Will our children look like Cain or like Abel?

CHAPTER 24

$\mathcal{T}$HEY HAD THOUGHT THEY WOULD NOT HAVE MUCH
to carry from the cave to the new refuge, but as they
walked along the bank of the river, woman, man, boys, and
girls looked like a line of marching ants.

Eve walked slowly, reluctantly. Not until she packed up
the shells, the bones, the small and large objects about her,
did she ask herself why it was she had agreed to leave that
familiar place that held in every cranny the memory of her
life. She had been amazed to find, in hiding places beneath
the rocks or in the pockets in the walls, animals' teeth, eroded
river rocks, the skeleton of a fish, a starfish, a plume from a
Phoenix, her children's dried umbilical cords. To see all those
things she had saved was to recognize the breadth and length
of the time that had passed since Elokim had banished them
from the Garden. She was overcome by the sadness of seeing
herself as if from a distance, as if the person who had treasured
all those things were only a memory. Images of her beginning
filled her mind as she indicated to her children what should

go or be left behind: dried skins, painted vessels, arrows and flint rocks, the fat, fecund clay figures that she had modeled as a kind of mockery during the days she was left alone, feeling like a sea on the verge of drowning. She realized she did not want to go. She had the premonition that when only silence and her drawings on the walls were left, the Eve that she had been in that place would dissolve, like the Garden. She debated whether to halt the feverish activity, share with Adam the lugubrious sound the empty cave had set echoing in her breast. She held back because of the enthusiasm of the others. They were eager to test the new refuge, to cross the footbridge they had built.

Adam overtook her on the path. He was carrying hide pouches filled with lances, hooks, arrowheads. He had noticed her slow steps, her bowed head, her reluctance.

"We can go back to the old cave anytime we want."

"But not to that time, Adam."

"Why would you want to go back to that time?" he asked. "To that solitude, to that bewilderment?"

"I don't know," she said. "It must be because we were younger there. It must be because the days seemed newer and we thought that we would be able to do more than devote ourselves to surviving. Sometimes I feel that surviving is the only thing we do."

The way he saw it, that was the challenge, he said. To demonstrate that they could survive.

Survive for what, she asked. What was the sense in being different from the animals if surviving was all there was? If she had eaten the forbidden fruit, it was because she thought there was something more.

Maybe there was, and the object was to discover it, he
said. She worried, she said, that they would never discover it.
You are sad, said Adam. Sadness is like smoke. It clouds your
vision.

They reached their refuge. Eve found that the busyness
of the children was contagious. The result of their labors was
good. They had tied slim tree trunks together with vines so
the footbridge would not be too heavy and they could draw
it back at nightfall. The trench was deep enough; the cave was
roomy and had more light. The animals could wander outside,
of course, but they could not get in.

It did not take long to get settled. Eve watched as each
person claimed a place for belongings. It was interesting to
see them define their space, arrange their treasures: the stones
they had labored on and refined bit by bit, the slim poles with
sharp tips for hunting, the instruments they used for cutting
and skinning. Luluwa had gold beads she treasured, straw
and grasses for making baskets. Aklia had bits of animal bone
for hooks and even implements for combing the knots from
sheep's wool. Abel, staffs and shepherd's canes to tend his flocks.
Cain the tools to sow the seeds he collected.

The moon turned red the first night they spent in the
new cave. Abel came in yelling. The sky is eating the moon,
he said. They all ran out. High in the firmament they saw the
full moon and a black mouth that was eating the edge. The
mouth opened wider and wider; a mouth of smoke blocking
out the splendor of the pale, defenseless sphere in the center
of the sky. Inexplicable. A sign, Adam thought. Out of concern
for Eve's anxieties, he had not carried out Elokim's mandate:
Abel with Luluwa, Cain with Aklia. Now the Other was going

to eat the moon. The nights would be blacker. He looked at Eve. Even in the darkness he could make out her pale face.

What is that? What is happening? the children asked. Waves of pain gripped Eve's stomach. Abel was right. No matter what she thought, this time she could not go against Elokim's wishes or dismiss Adam's dreams when in hers she wholeheartedly believed she saw and talked to the Serpent. Impossible to foresee what punishments Elokim would impose if they disobeyed once again, if she was again the one who instigated the man's disobedience. And yet, for days a dark premonition of misfortune had been spreading through her body. The moon took on the color of almonds. Reddish and round, it seemed posed upon a luminous pedestal high in a sky whose scintillating surface suddenly resembled the sea.

"It's a cloud," said Eve, to calm the twins. "It's as if it was cold and the moon wrapped itself in a cloud."

Adam walked over to her. He pointed to the sky and looked deep and long into her eyes. She understood.

"Do it," she said. "Speak with them."

Shortly after, they watched as the moon emerged from behind the coppery veil. The whole moon. Unscathed.

CHAPTER 25

To the north, following the trail of the bears, Adam had some time ago come across a mountain-enclosed valley of plenty where there was abundant hunting. He would take his sons there, talk with them, and inform them which of their sisters they would couple with. Eve wanted to protect Aklia. She was afraid that Cain would reject her as a substitute for Luluwa. She begged Adam to be sure to placate Cain before they returned.

They left a few days later, at daybreak. Eve went out to see them off, veiling her sorrow. She walked with them until the bright sun was high above. In the distance she could see the dark mountains beneath the unpredictable autumn sky. The ocher leaves lining the ground crunched beneath her footsteps. The water of the river was running dark, muddled by the rains that loosened the earth, the roots, the stones along its banks. When they took leave, Eve asked them to raise their hands when they reached the edge of the valley where the vegetation began to thin. That way she would be able to see them once more from a distance. She saw that her sons were puzzled, as they were used to her seeing them off without ceremony. Cain probably imagined she was doing it for him, she thought. Usually the three men did not go out together. It was rare for his father to ask him to come along. Adam and Abel usually went together and left Cain to go with the girls, or alone, looking for mushrooms, or for fertile land where he could plant his seeds. Clearly he was pleased that his father had asked him this time. Abel was also in good spirits. He loved his older brother. As a boy he always tagged along after him, imitating what he did. Often Abel's attempts to keep up with Cain ended in the inevitable accidents of childhood. Then Cain had to bear the wrath of his father, who scolded him for not taking care of his brother.

Eve waited on a promontory until after the men waved, the agreed-on salute, and disappeared into the distant vegetation. Then she sat down on the ground and burst into tears.

"Eve, Eve, don't cry."

The Serpent was sitting beside her. She was not crawling on the ground. She had the same form she'd had when Eve first saw her in the Garden of Eden.

"I dreamed about you," said Eve, amazed. "I dreamed about you as you were before, just as you are now. Did Elokim forgive you?"

"Yes."

"Do you think he will forgive us, too?"

"In his way, perhaps."

"What will happen to my children?"

"They will know Good and Evil."

"Will they suffer?"

"I told you that knowledge leads to suffering."

"You always say things so I can't understand you."

"I know no other way to talk."

"Tell me what evil is. Are you evil?"

The Serpent laughed.

"Me? Don't be ridiculous. Evil, Good, all the things there are, and will be, on this planet, originate right here: in you, in your children, in the generations to come. Knowledge and freedom are gifts that you, Eve, were the first to have and that your descendants will need to learn to use for themselves. Often they will blame you, but without those gifts their existence will be intolerable. The memory of Paradise will run in their blood, and if they succeed in understanding Elokim's game, and do not fall into his traps, they will close the circles of time and will recognize that the end can be equal to the beginning. To arrive there they will have nothing except freedom and knowledge."

"Are you saying that we will create Good and Evil on our own?"

"There's no one else. You are alone."

"And Elokim?"

"He will remember you from time to time, but what he forgets is as vast as what he remembers."

"We are alone."

"The day you accept that, you will be truly free. And now I must go."

"Will you fade away like the Garden? Will we see each other again?"

"I don't know."

"I think we will. I don't think you will forget me."

"Accept your solitude, Eve. Don't think of me, or of Elokim. Look around you. Use your gifts."

The Serpent evanesced in the afternoon air. Eve walked back the way she'd come. A strong wind was blowing. A storm was approaching. She wondered if they would endure the reality of being alone. Would they be that alone? She remembered the skins they had covered themselves with after they left the Garden, the wind that saved them from death when they had leaped from the mountain, the recent round, occult moon. Why those signs? Could it be that the Serpent wanted them to forget Elokim? It was true that if they were alone there would be no one but them to recognize Good and Evil, or to learn not to expect anything other than what they could provide for themselves, or to determine on their own, unaided, the purpose of life. Perhaps that was the freedom the Serpent was talking about. If Elokim had enticed them to take it, so he could forget them and go forth to create other worlds, then knowledge, everything that had happened since their expulsion from the Garden, would have been a gift and not a punishment; it would show he trusted that they, and those who issued forth from them and lived and multiplied and inhabited those expanses, would find for themselves, and would construct, a way of life that would console them for the certainty of death. But then how could she explain Elokim's mandates? Cain with Aklia, Abel with Luluwa? How would their freedom survive if they had to go against their hearts and obey unknown designs like those? Why did they always have to face the anxiety of such dilemmas—obey or disobey—and punishments? No, thought Eve. We are not alone. We would be better off if we were.

She returned to the cave. It was drizzling. She found Luluwa and Aklia weaving palms for the baskets they used to collect fruit. The silence of premonitions weighed over them. Ever if Eve or Adam had not said anything, Aklia and Luluwa had sensed that their father's trek with his sons was more than a hunting trip. They had bled. They were women. Life waited inside them.

"When will they be back?" they asked. "It won't be long," said Eve. She knew the hearts of the girls as well as she knew her own, but she could not bring herself to warn them of what lay ahead. She formed the words, chewed them, felt them move in her mouth, but something in her refused to speak them. She wanted the girls to be light of heart, wanted to delay their pain, to keep them wrapped in the tightly knit fabric that had enveloped their lives, and which now, as soon as words were spoken, would be ripped apart. She had never thought she would experience greater pain that what she had suffered when her children were born, but the pain that in recent days filled the air she breathed was as cruel as the pain locked in her memory. To know that there was precious little she could do to console the suffering they would endure brought a feeling of tightness to her chest. She dreamed herself following them along edge of precipices, roaring rivers, fires. She dreamed that her voice lay dead in her throat when she tried to warn them of the danger, the abysses, the tigers.

CHAPTER 26

*T*HE DAYS WENT BY. EVE WENT TO THE RIVER TO catch fish and crabs. The leaves were beginning to pale in the trees; there was a smell of wet earth, and a sad air of dying summer floated over the land. She squatted beside the riverbank with her palm basket to wait for fishes to come closer. She saw the gleam of the water, its transparency, the foam of the current milling around the edges of the rocks. Perhaps she was exaggerating her worries, she thought. What is happening to me? She did not recall a time when she had been so dispirited. Why not expect her sons to be content with their mates? They all would love each other. They were siblings. They would not have to separate, or to renounce love. Not knowing the intimacy of the flesh, perhaps they would bear the change with less pain than she foresaw. Perhaps it was the depth of her desire for Adam that led her to imagine an equal passion in Cain, in Luluwa. Abel would not object to his mate. Aklia preferred Cain. Much as she tried to convince herself, however, she could not imagine Luluwa and Cain resigned to ignore the instinct that had bound them together from the time they were young. She heard footsteps on the dried leaves. The Serpent, she thought. She looked up. It was Cain.

He came spilling over with words. Each with the impact of a sharp pebble. He threw them out in a hailstorm of feeling, without catching a breath. Jeering, passion, the cutting incisiveness of what he was saying was new in the air of the Earth. When did Cain's saliva turn bitter? Eve asked herself. She came out of the water, holding the basket, a couple of fishes jumping inside. She straightened her back and looked at him, eyes wide, the thumping of her heart pounding in her ears. Cain looked like he had been turned into stone. Hard. His face, hard, his mouth wide, down-turned, as if words took up more space than his teeth could hold. He spoke of beating, tearing, crushing, burying. He accused her for having given birth to him, for eating the fig, for losing Paradise, for allowing Adam to love only Abel. Idiot Abel. Only when he said "Luluwa" did his voice stumble, and he, aware of the effect, paused to recover the tone of injury and to describe, without a hint of brotherly love, Aklia's small, strange face that Eve, as long as she lived, could never consider any less beautiful than any of her other children's. It was hearing him say the things he said about Aklia that pulled Eve from her stunned, mute surprise.

"Go to the old cave, Cain, and do not come back until you are ready to ask for my forgiveness."

Straight as a staff, with her hand pointing into the distance, blazing with pain and fury, she watched Cain shrink before her icy stare. She heard his footsteps crushing leaves when he turned and marched off, striking rocks, tree branches, anything in his path, with the staff in his hands.

————

Adam's decision, Elokim's will, had like a cataclysm ripped apart the intimate fabric of their lives. Screams, imprecations, laments, Aklia's devastated face, and Abel's frightening silence were what Eve found when she came back from the river. Adam was pacing back and forth, bewildered.

"His rage reminded me of the time I killed the bear with my bare hands. Cain fell on me. Then he turned on Abel. Blind. Abel did nothing. He covered his face with his hands. I had to pull Cain off him. They both ended up sobbing. Cain came back running. Abel said nothing. He didn't speak all the way back here. I talked to him. I explained. He just looked at me. It was terrible," he said.

Eve led him from the cave. She took him to some rocks beneath the shade of a group of palm trees that grew in line with their new refuge. Still trembling, filled with anguish and anger. She sat down with her back against a stone. She didn't know about broken bones, but she imagined invisible bones that could fracture and make one crumple.

"This is like a new punishment."

"We obeyed. We saw the signs in the sky. You conceded."

"We lost Paradise. What will we lose this time?"

"I don't know, Eve. Perhaps this test is for them, for our children. Elokim must want to test their freedom, to know if they will obey him."

"They are very young. They won't understand."

Eve shook her head. She covered her face with her hands.

She could not cry. She wanted to protect her children. She could not resign herself to believe this was the trap that would make them lose their innocence. Liberty was a gift, the Serpent had said. But it seemed that Elokim himself did not understand freedom. He wanted them to be free, but he trapped them in those incomprehensible mandates. What was he made of? she asked herself. Of doubts, like us?

"What shall we do, Adam? How can we soothe Cain?"

"Time, Eve. Cain and Abel are brothers. Cain will understand that it wasn't Abel's decision," said Adam. "He will have to understand that there are bloods that must not be mixed. I will send them to make offerings together. You and I will make them see that they must reconcile, that they must understand Elokim's designs."

"As well as you and I understood?" Eve asked ironically.

The next day Cain still had not returned.

"I will send Aklia to look for Cain," said Adam.

"No! Don't send Aklia," she burst out. "I'm afraid he will do her harm. I will send Luluwa. He will listen to her. It will do the two of them good to talk."

Eve had Luluwa get up from the corner of the cave where she had been rolled in a ball since the previous night, her legs drawn to her chest, face between her knees, sobbing. She looked at Luluwa. She was so young. Her body and face had just left childhood behind; her body was still babbling a new language. Eve wondered what it was like for her children to grow and mature. Neither she nor Adam had experienced that. But she did know the fierce desire to disobey demands whose reasons one could not discern. And she also knew the consequences.

"Go look for Cain, Luluwa."

Aklia burst out crying. Abel's confused face was filled with quiet sorrow.

Luluwa went out to look for Cain. She went at midday and returned with him at dusk. It had been many hours. Eve looked at their faces cleansed of pain. They had disobeyed, she thought. They, too.

Cain knelt before Eve. He asked her forgiveness. Eve embraced him. She clasped him to her bosom. What will your punishment be, my son? she thought.

CHAPTER 27

*A*DAM ORDERED HIS SONS TO PREPARE THE GIFTS they would take as offering to Elokim.

Cain did not want to go with Aklia. When Luluwa left with Abel, Cain was squatting to prepare his tools. Luluwa looked at him as she went by. Her eyes were burning. Eve caught the exchange. She saw Cain's arm grow tense, saw his hand tighten around the handle of a spade.

The altar where Adam usually left his gift was near the old cave, south of the solitary mountain that rose amid the rocks of the reddish plain.

Cain hurried. His brother had the advantage because he had left ahead of him, but knowing Abel, Cain was sure he would take his time in choosing among the sheep of his flock. Cain went to the garden where he had sown squash. He cut the first ones he saw, and added a handful of wheat and a cluster of grapes. He moved with haste and was able to reach the site just as Abel and Luluwa were arriving. His brother was carrying a sacrificed sheep over his shoulder. His best, of course.

It was handsome and fat and the blood of its slashed throat was spattered across Abel's neck and chest.

Cain was the first to stand before Adam's altar. He set down his offering. Then Abel stepped forward. He attempted to lay the sheep beside his brother's offering, but Cain stood in his way.

"I am sorry, Abel. You will have to look for a different place to lay your offering"

"I thought we would do it together."

"You were mistaken."

"But there's enough room."

Cain pushed him. He tightened the muscles on the right side of his body and threw his weight against Abel hard enough to make his brother lose his balance.

"Cain!" exclaimed Luluwa.

"You be quiet," Cain shouted at her.

Abel looked at his brother, incredulous. He looked him up and down. He stepped aside and began to pick up stones to make his own altar. His brusque movements betrayed his astonishment and discomfort.

Cain was watching his brother out of the corner of his eye. Luluwa was sitting on a rock, her back bent over, her arms crossed at the waist, her foot jiggling nervously, making designs in the dirt.

Very soon Abel had improvised an altar, on which he laid the lamb. Then he knelt. He was very quiet; his eyes were closed.

Cain knelt, too. He heard his heart throbbing in his arms, in his legs, spurred by the stimulus of a rage that completely filled him and prevented him from thinking or praying.

The darkening sky announced a downpour. Luluwa looked at the black, ominous clouds on the horizon. She felt the wind rear its head among the trees.

Suddenly a blaze of lightning blinded them. They breathed in the odor of burned flesh. The lightning had struck precisely on Abel's lamb, consuming it. Nothing was left on the rocks except the outline of the animal and a pile of black ash.

Abel looked at Cain. He smiled beatifically.

"Praised be Elokim," he said loudly, and prostrated himself.

Accursed be Elokim, thought Cain; may you, Elokim, be accursed. You favor my brother, just as my father does.

Cain had never heard the Voice. When he did hear it reverberating in his head, he began to tremble. He heard the remonstrance clearly: "Why do you curse me, Cain? Why are you sad? If you are heedful, and just, I will accept your offering as well. When you insult me you insult yourself."

Cain ran off, shamed, contrite. He did not stop until he found Eve.

He laid his head on her breast as he had when he was a child.

"The Voice spoke to me. It spoke to me, the Voice," he repeated. "I heard it, Mother. I heard it."

Eve cradled him. She calmed him. Cain's confusion was a ripping in her heart. All her other children had at one time or other heard the Voice. All except Cain. Now that he had heard it, she intuited that along with his terror he felt finally that he had at least been taken into account. Adam, who had just come down to the refuge, learned through Eve what had happened. He saw Cain held tight in her arms. Before he could react, Abel and Luluwa came into the cave, slipping hurriedly along the steps. Cain leaped from his mother's arms and went to stand in a corner, his back against the wall, his face sullen. Abel could not contain his emotion. Elokim himself had taken his offering, wrapped in a ray of light, he said jubilantly. They all had to have seen it, he exclaimed. "Of the sheep I laid on the stone of the offerings, only a few ashes remain."

Luluwa not only corroborated what Abel said, but also reported the altercation between the brothers. She reproached Cain. That wasn't the way he would gain Elokim's understanding, she said. Cain's eyes glittered in the darkness. Impenetrable. He said nothing. He allowed them to celebrate Abel and censure him. Aklia cast an oblique glance at him. She tried to sit by his side, to take his hand. He brushed her away with a cuff that no one felt more than she did.

Cain did not sleep that night. He paced outside the cave, in the moonlight. Eve looked out and saw the anguished silhouette, the fury of his steps. She went back to lie beside Adam, beset with worry and unable to sleep.

The next day, Cain went with Aklia to the field. Adam thought that he was more tranquil. Luluwa was agitated until they returned. Eve could not quiet the noise inside her. It must be the autumn, she thought, everything slowly dying: the trees stripped of their leaves, the nights growing shorter, the hooting of the owls, the sound of steps on the leaves, steps that do not exist except in my imagination. The world was tense, crouched down; it reminded her of how the air had stilled after she had eaten of the fruit of the Tree of Knowledge of Good and Evil.

Eve cuddled Aklia. "Cain doesn't love me," she said. "Not Cain, not Abel, not Luluwa, not my father. Who am I, Mother?

What is my destiny? I see the bands of monkeys and often I want to go with them. I look like them. They would accept me."

"But you are not one of them, Aklia."

"I would be more comfortable. They wouldn't reject me."

"What do you know, daughter?"

"I know that Cain will not be my mate. What do you know, Mother?"

"I know you are not a monkey."

"And what would it matter if I were? At least I would know what I am."

"But you can think."

"How do you know they can't?"

"They merely survive. They do not speak."

"And that is bad?"

"I don't know, Aklia. Sometimes I don't know what is Good and what is Evil. Please be calm. Go to sleep."

Eve thought a long time about what Aklia had said. Looking at her face, she remembered the monkey that had invited her to climb a tree in the wooded valley, and then had shown her the way back to the cave. She held Aklia close. Silently, she wept. Aklia's hair grew wet with her mother's tears.

CHAPTER 28

*I*SOLATED FROM THE OTHERS, CAIN DEVOTED HIM-
self to his seeds. He harvested lentils and wheat; he turned
the earth for the plants that would come up in the spring.
He went back to the cave at inopportune times. He watched
Luluwa and Abel. He refused to speak to Aklia.

Adam avoided sinking into the sadness that threatened
them all. He had survived till now and would continue to survive. He and Eve would reproduce if it turned out that their
children did not. With time, Cain would temper his restlessness.
If Cain's mother and father had endured the loss of the Garden,
then Cain, too, would have to endure. He would have to wait.
Time passes and carries off nonconforming behavior with it;
one accepted what one could not change. Eve had circles beneath her eyes. She slept very little.

The routine of the hunt was restored. Winter was coming
and they had to prepare for the cold, dark nights, for the chill
earth and naked trees. Abel and Adam again went out together.

Aklia, Luluwa, and Eve brought mushrooms, herbs, and fish to the cave. The nights were tense, filled with sounds and footsteps. Eve closed her eyes tight and refused to see who was walking around. She forced Adam to stay quiet. One early morning she thought she heard a band of monkeys at the other end of the footbridge. She sat up and looked for Aklia, but couldn't see her; however, by morning Aklia was there as she always was. It was a dream, Eve told herself.

A day came when Cain emerged from his aloofness. Eve thought that maybe she would be able to sleep as she once had, not the fragile sleep interrupted by sounds that she had no way of knowing were real or imaginary. She saw Cain go to Abel, and saw them talking, and had to leave to hide her tears of relief.

The following morning the brothers left together. Eve watched them go in an air of peace. Bent over the channel he was digging to divert water from the river and shorten the distance they had to go to satisfy their thirst, Adam smiled at his wife.

The day was light and crystalline. Toward dusk, Eve was painting vessels; Aklia was sharpening hooks; Adam was finishing the channel for the water. The sound of rustling leaves, of someone running, made them look up.

Luluwa burst from the bushes, panting.

What was it in Luluwa's eyes that had shaken her so? Eve sprang up anxiously.

"What happened?" she asked.

Luluwa opened her mouth. No sound came out.

"What happened?" her mother repeated.

Adam and Aklia left what they were doing.

"Cain struck Abel. Abel isn't making a sound. He is on the ground, with his eyes open."

Luluwa began telling them. She said that early in the afternoon, as she was weaving baskets, she saw that it was futile to try to set a rhythm between her hands and her thoughts, and decided it would be better to go look for Cain and Abel. Worried, she left without notifying anyone because she felt whirring insects buzzing in her head, and a flock of disoriented birds flapping their wings in her breast. She ran as fast as her legs would carry her to the wheat plantings. She asked herself where Cain might have taken Abel, because she did not find them there, or up river where the mushrooms grew, or where the squash lifted their orange heads. She wondered about the old cave, the fig trees, the peaches. She ran on, panting. As she went, she startled monkeys in the trees, wild pigs. In her course, thorns scored her skin. When she reached the little grove of peach trees, she picked up the scent of Cain. He had been there, but he had gone on. She sniffed the air, circled the solitary mountain, climbed up on some rocks to see if from there she could catch sight of her brothers. She saw something lying on a small promontory. She ran that way, calling to Cain not to leave, to wait for her. When she got there, she bent over to ease the sharp pain shooting through her ribs from having run so fast.

"I thought that Abel was sleeping stretched out on the ground, and that Cain was by his side watching him sleep. But then I heard Cain's moans. I saw him sitting with his head between his knees. He was rocking back and then forward with his hands laced behind his neck. The instant he saw me, he yelled. He began to sob. What happened to Abel, Cain? And he told me: He is dead, Luluwa. I killed him.

He is dead Luluwa, I killed him. He is dead, Luluwa, I killed him. He is dead, Luluwa, I killed him. Eve heard the phrase and all the words in the world other than those disappeared. She wanted to think, and only *He is dead, Luluwa, I killed him.* She wanted to speak, and only *He is dead Luluwa, I killed him.* She kept seeing those words, seeing the image that Luluwa described: Abel on the ground and Cain saying that over and over.

Luluwa continued: You killed him? I asked, unable to understand. I thought, we've never seen anyone die. I thought Cain was mistaken. Then I knelt beside Abel and I began to call to him. I saw the blood beneath his head. A red aureole. I saw that Abel was staring at the sky. I shook him. I begged him to wake up. Abel was cold, icy cold, like the water in the river. He doesn't wake up, Cain told me. He told me he had already tried. He told me that he did not hear any sound inside Abel. He shouted that he had killed him.

"And he killed him," moaned Luluwa, herself sobbing. "He killed him. It's true. I saw him. He's dead. He doesn't move. He doesn't speak. He stares straight before him. And he is cold. Cain killed him. Cain killed him! He didn't mean to, but he killed him. Poor Cain. What will become of us now? Where is Abel? Where is death? What will we do to make him come back?"

None of them had died yet, Eve thought. They couldn't die, Adam thought. Eve remembered the Serpent. It was not easy to die, she'd said. Elokim will not let that happen, Adam told himself. Eve and he a long time ago had jumped from the peak of the mountain, thinking they would die, only to fall in the river without a scratch.

"Come, Luluwa. Take us to your brothers."

CHAPTER 29

*T*HE FOUR OF THEM RAN WITHOUT STOPPING. THEY ran through the autumn countryside. It was growing dark. In the sky the clouds were blazing in the red light of sunset; the dark and hostile earth returned the sound of their feet pounding rhythmically on the ground. A pack. A terrified pack. As they passed, birds flew up from the trees. Animals caught the scent of their anguish. None came near them.

He is dead, Luluwa, I killed him. Eve wanted to erase the words, but they were as loud as the sound of heels thudding one after the other on the path. And if it was true? And if Cain had killed Abel? They all knew how to kill. Even she did. Fish died in her baskets. Their tails flailed against its sides when they were out of the water. But kill another like themselves? How could Cain not have known his strength? Luluwa told them that Cain had struck his brother with a rock. That was how Adam killed rabbits. And that was how he told her he had killed the bear that mangled his dog. What had Adam done, what had she done, when they killed their first creature? What cruel forces had they unleashed in order to survive? In order to eat? And why had Elokim so disposed? Had he known what he was doing? And had it been done with the abandon he displayed in painting the sky, in conceiving flowers and the wings of the birds? Was he thinking at all? Since he did not live the way they did, how could he decide their lives, decide what could or could not be?

Luluwa pointed to the promontory. They climbed. Aklia moaned and stumbled along. Eve saw her putting her weight on her hands to push forward, to move more rapidly.

"Don't hurt your hands, Aklia."

Aklia looked at her with gentle eyes. She said nothing. She made only a sad, high sound.

Adam saw the figure of Abel lying flat on the ground. He had killed too many animals not to recognize the signs. But he ran to Abel to touch him. He was the first to rest his head on Abel's chest. His weeping was hoarse, immense. The air absorbed his wailing. It was a call, an admission of defeat.

Eve approached Abel slowly. Her legs were trembling. She recalled the feeling of having Abel in her womb. The slippery wax and blood on his little body. Her eyes stopped at the boy's feet. They were stained, flat, large. The toes. Her children's little toes. When they were born nothing else had so filled her with wonder. The feet and the tiny ears, the lobes curved like shells. She went closer. She saw his staring eyes. She bent down and touched his eyelids to close them. She did it without thinking. Knowledge of Good and Evil.

Beautiful Abel. Sleeping. She stroked his forehead. His skin so cold. Sadness spread slowly through her body; it was as if water were filling her body until she couldn't breathe.

She dropped down beside Abel's head. She caressed him. She wanted to put her arms around him, to hold him to her bosom, to hug him tightly, console him. How lonely he would be now, she thought. More lonely than they, who were themselves so lonely. Adam was weeping. His lament issued from a place that seemed to be not in him but in the earth itself. She took Abel's head and laid it in her lap.

"Help me, Adam, help me hold him. Put him in my arms."

Adam helped her. She cradled her son. She rocked him. There was no way to weep for this pain, she thought, tears running down her cheeks, spilling onto her breasts. She clasped Abel to her. "Where is your life, Abel? Why aren't you moving?"

He was so heavy, so forlorn. She touched his head. The wound in his skull. It was not bleeding any longer. She felt the void in her womb. She felt the absence of her son like a emptying out of herself. Only water flooding through her. Water, choking her until she was able to emit a deep moan, to let go in the pain of knowing that she would never again see Abel alive. Never.

She saw Aklia leaping about, Luluwa moaning.

"Where is Cain?" Eve asked. "Where is my son Cain?"

"I don't know," Luluwa answered. "I don't know."

"Look for him, Luluwa. Look for him so he can help us carry Abel to the cave. We can't leave him here."

It was deep into the night. Adam lit fires. One on each side of Abel, Adam and Eve sat by their son beneath a dark, starry sky.

Aklia had fallen asleep.

"I remember when I became aware that I was," said Adam.

"I remember, and I think it would have been better never to exist."

"I remember when I ate of the fruit of the Tree. I should not have done that."

"Abel would never have died. It all started with you, Eve." He looked up. He looked at her with grieving rancor.

"Without me, Abel would never have existed," she returned. "We wouldn't have loved. The life that had to be began with me. All I did was fulfill my destiny."

"And death began."

"I gave life, Adam. The one who began to kill was you."

"So we could survive."

"I'm not blaming you, but once we accepted that it was necessary to kill in order to survive, we allowed necessity to rule our conscience, and we let cruelty in. And now look how cruelty has come to roost in our lives."

"It was inevitable. As inevitable as your eating the fruit."

"If Elokim hadn't forced us to cross the twins between the pairs, maybe this wouldn't have happened."

"Why did he create us, Eve? I don't believe that I can suffer more than I am suffering now."

"The Serpent said that Elokim made us to see whether we would be able to return to the beginning and regain Paradise."

"So perhaps we are not the beginning?"

"From what she told me, in the Garden we were the image of what Elokim wanted to see at the end of his creation. When we ate the fig, he altered the direction of time. Now to go back to that point of departure, our children and the children of their children, the generations that will come after us, will have to begin all over, to regress. That was what she said."

"And what will we have to regress to?"

"I don't know, Adam. I think that we will end up living in a pack. Maybe the future lies in Aklia. Maybe that is why you find her strange. Maybe she is the past that we never knew."

"Aklia, so innocent."

"And essential."

"But she would still have to kill."

"Cain killed."

Eve said nothing.

Finally she said, "I mourn that son as much as this one."

"Don't you believe that we must punish him?"

"Punish him? I assure you that no punishment we impose will be as harsh as what he will suffer on his own. He will go away with Luluwa. I foresee it. I believe that, like you and me, they have already disobeyed."

CHAPTER 30

$\mathcal{I}$T WAS NEARLY DAWN WHEN CAIN RETURNED WITH
Luluwa. He prostrated himself before Adam and Eve.

"I never meant to kill Abel," he moaned. "I didn't know the
weight of my hand."

"Get up," said Eve.

Cain stood. Eve saw the deep circle on his brow. Crimson.
Raw flesh. A burn.

"Who marked you?" Adam asked.

"Elokim."

"How?" Eve asked. "Tell us."

"Abel said that he would be a good father for Luluwa's
children, that I would be happy with Aklia," he sobbed. "I told
him that Luluwa and I were a single being and that neither of
us could exist without the other. But he said that it was the
will of Elokim that he should procreate with Luluwa. I struck
him. I didn't know that my blows would kill him. I hid. Then
I heard Elokim's voice. He asked me about Abel. He asked me
about Abel! He who knows everything. I was enraged," he

wept. "'Am I my brother's keeper?' I replied. He said that my brother's blood had cried out to him. And he cursed me! The earth would never yield its fruit to me, he decreed. He would make me a fugitive who would wander through the world. I begged him, I prostrated myself. I told him that my punishment was greater than I could bear. The animals will slay me; those who come later will slay me. Then he made this mark on my forehead. They would see the mark and they would not slay me, he said. If they did, his vengeance would fall upon them sevenfold."

Cain started to throw himself into Adam's arms. He was sobbing, trembling. Adam pushed him away. Eve took him in her arms, but she could not make her heart embrace him. Cain left them.

Luluwa threw herself down. She beat her head upon the ground. She thought about Abel, about the body of Cain, which only days before she had felt so deep inside her. She thought about how she loved him, about the solitude that would accompany them and the loneliness they would have to live in. She wept with a weeping that ululated like the wind, as if a storm had taken possession of her and its lightning and thunder were destroying her.

Among them, they carried Abel's body to the old cave, where he had been born. Eve cleaned the blood from his head. She remembered the first time she had washed him in the stream. How soft and pliable and warm he was when he had just emerged from her womb; how stiff and cold he was now. She let the air out of her lungs. She heard herself howling like a wolf. Her pain was untouched, like a new wound that nothing could heal.

Adam burned aromatic resins at his son's side. They thought of burning the body on the bonfire so the smoke of the sacrifice would rise up to Elokim. Where were you, Elokim, when my children were killing each other? Adam cried out in silence. Luluwa begged them to put Abel in the ground. Since Abel had not had children, his body could at least become a tree and would sweeten the fruit. Adam imagined his son's smile appearing among the leaves of a tree. Dust you are and unto dust shall you return. Fertile dust.

They had to bury Abel three times. The earth that had never known the death of a human, once, twice, returned his remains. They closed the hole and it reopened. It was not until the third time, until Adam and Eve prostrated themselves and asked the earth to receive their son, that it closed over Abel's body and held him forever.

CHAPTER 31

C AIN HAD TO LEAVE FOR THE LAND OF NOD.
He said that was what Elokim had ordered him to do.

Adam refused to wait to see him leave. He returned alone to the cave without memories. He had only daughters left, he said. His two sons were dead.

Eve reproached his harshness. With his own hands, to avenge the death of his dog, he had killed a bear that was defending her cub. He knew the irrational rage of losing what he loved.

"May the time you dream of, Eve, the time without cruelty, come to pass."

"Forgive Cain."

Adam did not yield. She remembered having once wondered if Elokim had formed him of a slab from a mountain.

Eve stayed with her children in the cave of the drawings.

Cain and Luluwa barely exchanged a word. They prepared the tools and seeds and coverings they would take with them to the east of the Garden of Eden. Cain had discovered those lands in one of his wanderings. It was green, he said. Even if nothing sown by his hands gave fruit, Luluwa would not be hungry or thirsty.

Aklia had not spoken since the death of Abel. Curled up in the hollow of a rock, in the dark depths of the cave, she did not answer Eve's calls. When Eve went near her, she saw Aklia's sweet, terrified eyes. Her speech forgotten, Aklia also seemed to have lost reason and conscience in order to surrender herself with no misgivings to live as a simian. Eve watched Aklia closely. She barely slept, afraid that her daughter would go off with the troop of monkeys that prowled around the cave at night.

One morning, Eve observed Cain and Luluwa washing in the stream, preparing to set off for the uncertainty of their vagabond lives. She saw Cain's hands and felt as if she were again touching the deep wound in Abel's head. Without ceasing to love him, she wanted difficulties for him that would force him to humility and shame. She possessed the terrible knowledge of her son's being; she knew the precise instant in which his branches twisted and his roots thirsted, never to be watered. She understood the origins but did not come to an understanding of the violence. That violence, especially. The violence that made him capable of killing his brother.

Luluwa sobbed when she bid Aklia good-bye, but her younger sister merely looked at her. Aklia lifted her arms, not to embrace Luluwa, but to touch her own head; her brilliant, tearless eyes fixed on her sibling with curiosity. Luluwa did not weep when she said good-bye to Eve. She was proud, reluctant to admit fragility. She protected herself behind her beauty, but, more than anything, she loved Cain and did not want to show any fissure between them in front of her mother.

Eve watched the blurred figures of her children growing smaller as they crossed the plain, and she missed Adam. She had hoped he would come.

Pain left her immobilized. Gradually her staring eyes focused on the cave with the walls covered with paintings. She thought of the trail those figures had imprinted on her heart before they existed on stone. Every rough or graceful symbol recaptured for her a part of her past she had wanted to save from oblivion. Because following Abel's death, her whole being was open and unprotected, Eve recapitulated her uncommon existence without falseness or invention. She recognized that despite having been ripped from Paradise, she and Adam had brought much more than memories from it. It kept following them, circling and floating over their lives. They had never lost it. They would not lose it as long as its indelible traces were left drawn inside them.

The Serpent appeared one more time.

Before going back to Adam, Eve took Aklia to know the sea. In only a few days, her daughter's hair had again covered her cheeks. The skin of her hands and her long, delicate feet had hardened, turning a dark tone. She seemed determined to let the night inhabit her. She walked holding Eve's hand, docile and awkward, bereft of words. At times along the way, she dropped Eve's hand and ran on her own, putting part of her weight on her arms. She was dazzled by the sea. Happy, she leaped about over the sand and covered her eyes with her arm to shield them from its splendor. Eve let her play, and threw shells for her to pick up.

Eve sat down on the rock on which she'd dreamed she had seen a woman clothed in feathers, whose face had turned into her own. She heard the voice of the Serpent before seeing her.

"Look at little Aklia. The past and the future are running with her along the beach."

"What do you mean?"

"She has returned to innocence, Eve, an innocence preceding the Garden, the antecedent to the Garden. History has jumped from you to her now, and a long, slow time is about to begin."

"I don't know if I believe you. Why Aklia? Why not Cain and Luluwa? Why not Adam and me?"

"We have all fulfilled our designs, Eve. Just as you have drawn the codes of your past on the walls of the cave, Elokim has drawn on us the symbols with which humanity will come to know itself."

"And Aklia?"

"Aklia is Elokim's reality. We are his dreams."

"You said that in the beginning was the end."

"The end for Aklia's descendants will be to reach the beginning. To recognize it as the persistent memory of what they thought they would find in making and destroying their own history."

"They will return to the Garden? And then what? Will they wonder what there is beyond it? Will they be bored?"

"Perhaps not. They will not suffer the blindness of innocence, the desire to know. They will not need to taste the forbidden fruit to know Good and Evil. They will have it in them. They will know that the only real Paradise will be the one in which they possess freedom and knowledge."

"Do you think they will ever be truly free? Do you think that Elokim will allow them that?"

"Existence is a game to Elokim. If your species finds harmony, Elokim will move on. I believe that secretly he wants to be granted the gift of forgetfulness so he can be freed from the solitude of his power. With that he will be able to go on to construct other universes."

"Will you go with him?"

"I will if your species succeeds in understanding the signs. I will go if it happens that he and I do not end up as victims of our own creations."

Eve looked at the Serpent with sadness. As she watched, the skin of scales became covered with white feathers, and the flat face grew finer. Within a few seconds the soft, brilliant plumage covered the Serpent completely. Again, as in her old dream, Eve saw her face reflected in that of the creature, instants before the Serpent dissolved forever.

Eve called to Aklia. She took her hand and began the walk back to the cave. They left the scent of the sea behind. They crossed gentle hills. They spent the night embraced beneath a ledge of rocks. At dawn they descended to the thick vegetation in which Eve had been lost long ago. The gold of autumn illuminated the foliage of the oaks. Eve held Alika's hand tight. Restless, Aklia looked toward the treetops. She made little leaps. She scratched her head.

Eve saw the troop of large, graceful monkeys swinging through the branches. Her eyes grew moist. How much I have lost! she thought.

Aklia released Eve's hand. Before she let her go, Eve bent down and hugged Aklia to her heart. "Remember me, Aklia," she said. "Remember everything you have lived. Someday you will speak again. Go now. Run, daughter, run and recover Paradise!"

Eve walked on alone. A light drizzle began to fall over the world. And then came the rain.

Managua–La Finca–Santa Monica

2007

Long Branch Public Library
732-222-3900
www.lmxac.org/longbranch

Author: Belli, Gioconda, 1948-
Item ID: 37834001457034
User name: POVEROMO, NADINE
Title: Infinity in the palm of her hand : a nove
l of Ada
User ID: 27834000068727
Date due: 12/8/2010,23:59
Date charged: 10/18/2010,10:50

NO RENEWALS-MOVIES & MAGAZINES
CARD # REQ'D FOR ACCOUNT INFO.

ACKNOWLEDGMENTS

*A*s I wrote in the introduction to this novel, I owe the discovery of Adam and Eve's lost story to a find I made in a library. The library belonged to Lou Castaldi, my father-in-law, an extraordinary human being who should have lived forever but who died two years ago, at age ninety-six. I want to believe his spirit is still hovering around us, and that somehow he will read these words. I want to thank him, not only for whatever made him own the books that fired up my imagination but for being an inspiration. Like Eve, he would have chosen knowledge over eternity. His curiosity and vitality brimmed over and were a joy to behold. I am grateful to life for allowing me to know him and be close to him.

I wouldn't have met Lou had it not been for Charlie, his son, my husband, the father of our daughter Adriana and stepfather to Maryam, Camilo, and Melissa, my children. I have shared more than twenty years of my life with Charlie and we have sailed gales and calm seas, thanks to a love that has kept us mightily entertained, amused, and surprised at each other's mutations. I thank him for tolerating my escapes into fantasy worlds inhabited by creatures whose voices and shapes populate my fiction. I thank him for keeping our lives forever varied and interesting, for cooking amazing meals, being a hands-on, steadfast father, and never trying to curtail my independence.

I want to thank some of the friends who offered me solace and solidarity while I wrote this book: Joan Peters, whose notes are always insightful and helpful; Margie Schroth, who made sure I was comfortable at the HF Bar Ranch in Wyoming, where I wrote the final chapters of this novel; to Maria Morrison, my wonderful friend, who is so generous with her encouragement and knows how to tell me the truth without depressing me; to Viviana Suaya and my sister Lavinia for their soulful support; to John Carlin, Ana Cristina Rossi, and my many friends in Nicaragua, for celebrating my choices and making me believe I had done something worthwhile.

I thank my kids for putting up with me. Each and every one of them is an inspiration for my life and my work. Each makes me proud. Bringing them into this world and raising them has made my life more meaningful, rich, and worthwhile.

I want to thank my translator extraordinaire, Margaret Sayers-Peden, "Petch," for her patience, her good humor, her warmth, and understanding. Working with her was a joy and a learning experience.

I am incredibly lucky and blessed to have amazing editors: Elena Ramírez in Spain and René Alegría in the United States. Their support, advice, and enthusiasm for this book helped me give it my best effort. I thank my agent, Guillermo Schavelzon, for caring so much for my work and believing that yes, I can; to Bonnie Nadell, my U.S. agent, because even when she tells me what I don't want to hear, she does it with grace and good humor.